HACKNEY LIBRARY SERVICES

Please return this book to any library in Hackney, on or
before the last date stamped. Fines may be charged if it is late.
Avoid fines by renewing the book (subject to it NOT being reserved).

Call the renewals line on 020 8356 2539

People who are over 60, under 18 or registered disabled
are not charged fines.

02/20

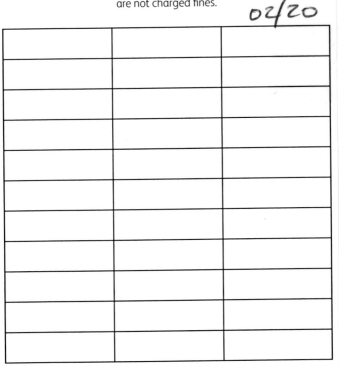

⊖ Hackney

PJ42014

LONDON B

9130

D0547612

SPECIAL MESSAGE TO READERS

THE ULVERSCROFT FOUNDATION
(registered UK charity number 264873)

was established in 1972 to provide funds for research, diagnosis and treatment of eye diseases. Examples of major projects funded by the Ulverscroft Foundation are:-

- The Children's Eye Unit at Moorfields Eye Hospital, London
- The Ulverscroft Children's Eye Unit at Great Ormond Street Hospital for Sick Children
- Funding research into eye diseases and treatment at the Department of Ophthalmology, University of Leicester
- The Ulverscroft Vision Research Group, Institute of Child Health
- Twin operating theatres at the Western Ophthalmic Hospital, London
- The Chair of Ophthalmology at the Royal Australian College of Ophthalmologists

You can help further the work of the Foundation by making a donation or leaving a legacy. Every contribution is gratefully received. If you would like to help support the Foundation or require further information, please contact:

THE ULVERSCROFT FOUNDATION
The Green, Bradgate Road, Anstey
Leicester LE7 7FU, England
Tel: (0116) 236 4325

website: www.foundation.ulverscroft.com

COOKING UP A STORM

Artist and entrepreneur Amy Chambers runs a quirky but popular café and art studio in Derbyshire with her sister Lorna. When they win the chance to be mentored by a celebrated business angel who will assist with their expansion, it's an exciting prospect — until Amy realises it will put her head to head with the country's most renowned celebrity chef and global gourmet, Mal Donaldson, who takes no prisoners. Can Mal find a way to convince her that together they have the perfect ingredients for lasting happiness?

JUDY JARVIE

COOKING UP
A STORM

Complete and Unabridged

LINFORD
Leicester

First published in Great Britain in 2018

First Linford Edition
published 2019

A catalogue record for this book is available
from the British Library.

ISBN 978–1–4448–4226–5

Published by
F. A. Thorpe (Publishing)
Anstey, Leicestershire

Set by Words & Graphics Ltd.
Anstey, Leicestershire
Printed and bound in Great Britain by
T. J. International Ltd., Padstow, Cornwall

This book is printed on acid-free paper

1

'Stop it!' Amy Chambers beckoned her elder sister urgently away from the window. 'He'll think we're crazy. And even though you definitely are, I'd rather not shove it in his face straight away.'

Lorna's expression displayed her adrenaline-hyped state as she peeked between the blinds. 'He looks better than on television, if that's possible. Taller and definitely more dishy. And he has a tan. I wonder where he's been filming?'

Amy knew; she'd read about it online. He'd filmed a street food series in Thailand after judging an Australian chef contest. Mal Donaldson was a busy and talked-about man, she'd discovered.

He was also the country's dishy, darling chef célèbre with the book deals, restaurant kudos and TV shows on regular repeat to prove it.

Bodily pulling Lorna back, Amy seized

her attention. 'Yes, he's the nation's pin-up chef. But you need to quit displaying this embarrassing adulation stuff. Especially as your husband is just outside. We don't want duelling among the radishes!'

Lorna batted the comment away. 'Harry knows my interest is harmless and purely professional.' She laughed and flipped her short, red-streaked hair. 'Anyway he'd never harm his precious veggies! He didn't win that organic produce award without treating them like precious rarities that need love, care and attention.'

Amy pushed her point. 'Still. Are you twelve or thirty? Stop peeking at our special visitor before he catches you.'

She often never knew whether to laugh at Lorna or push her somewhere for safety. Her loose-cannon tendencies jarred with Amy's introversion. Amy might be the younger, but Lorna was lack-of-filter personified.

Lorna was great — she just did everything at maximum setting without scruples. While Amy was a steadying influence, Lorna was all wild fashion and noisy chaos. The fact that she was a brilliant café cook in her own right was her key redeeming feature.

Lorna pulled a face. 'Are we up to this? We're just a tiny café in the wilds of Derbyshire. He's accomplished and famous. Big time, sis. What if he's not impressed — hates my menu? What if I fluff the whole gig up?'

'As if! You really think that's likely?'

Amy gestured around her. Their rustic organic café may be small-scale, but it had an aerodrome backdrop that drew gasps. They brought many repeat customers, and not just for their renowned aromatic coffee blend.

'We have a vision. If he doesn't like it, he knows where the door is.' She gazed out to the airfield that adjoined High Marsh Hideaway.

Would they take off? Or nose-dive? They could only try their best and see.

They'd put everything into their contest entry. Then they'd got short-listed — even won. Surely the hard part was over?

So why was Amy's stomach in more tangled knots than the monkey puzzle tree by the gate?

Amy dismissed her own misgivings and opted for bluster. 'We have a lottery grant in our favour. And he's supposed to be our business angel. You have to believe we're going to succeed. Believe and conquer.'

She glanced to the garden where Lorna's husband Harry Davey surveyed their organic vegetable plots. Mal Donaldson was now walking up the path and introducing himself. It made Amy gulp and try to swallow, difficult when your mouth had dried like the desert.

Harry was first to intercept him. Now her nerves kicked in big time and she felt overwhelmed by the moment.

No, they weren't just a café — they were a café plus an organic store and veg delivery business, art studio, educational space and craft shop. Now they hoped to expand into a community hub and education centre too. And if this famous business mentor couldn't guide them, nobody stood a chance.

He had a string of restaurants and his name on hotel menus across the globe, not to mention cruise ships. He was every business owner's dream boost.

'He's got all the right experience and contacts — an ideal guy to lead the way.' She knew she was repeating the script like a robot. Convincing herself.

Amy also told herself her butterflies were normal. They weren't because the man was gorgeous, talented and off-the-scale gifted. In the flesh, even from the window, he was way more gorgeous than she'd banked on. Mal Donaldson was a household name that garnered attention and female fans.

As well as shaky knees. Especially hers.

'Ever consider we might be capable of raising our game?' Amy knelt to shove logs in the café burner to make the space as welcoming as it could be. Then she stacked the basket in place. It may have wood-notch cabin walls and a reclaimed timber floor but it had high beams and great views through a glass wall that stretched to take in the whole airfield. Plus space to sit twenty comfortably to enjoy the produce from their inviting kitchen that was the heart of the place.

'You're right,' Lorna muttered. 'It's the nerves talking.'

Amy briefly hugged her sister.

'Seriously. We're a good bet, sis. Well, Harry's won the most awards. But we do a mean job of keeping up with his prowess.' Amy pushed her curly chestnut hair back from her damp brow.

Lorna squeaked, 'Quick! He's coming in.'

She jumped for cover behind the counter and almost went all her length on the tiled floor.

Amy snagged a spare apron to hide any paint stains on her shirt she may have missed, then ran to stand beside Lorna.

'Act confident. And we won't tell Harry you've got the hots for Mal.'

6

'Tell him. I love it when a man gets all proprietorial and caveman on me!'

Amy suppressed her instinct to laugh.

'I can just see Harry as a caveman. That's a mental image I won't be able to erase from my brain now.'

'Have you seen Mal's car?' Lorna stage whispered. 'A motorised mortgage. Mal Donaldson must earn a fortune.'

'I'll only be impressed if he takes us full speed to our next level. It's his wisdom we need.'

At that moment Harry entered through the side door wearing his familiar warm smile. Mal Donaldson, a face Amy felt she knew well but only from his TV legacy, followed behind. He ducked under the low beams in the entranceway and she was struck by his height and dark longer-length hair, and easy manner. He raised an eyebrow and then extended a hand.

'Hello. Here at last. You ladies really are out in the wilds. I love this place!'

'Welcome, I'm Amy.' She forced a

smile as their hands touched. The contact zapped. His fingers were warm but surprisingly calloused for a man who worked indoors. Amy felt something in her stomach melt and fizz.

Mal took charge.

'Hi, and you must be Lorna. Chef extraordinaire.' He seized her hand. 'I'm just a visiting chef — here to bask in your glory.'

'As if! An honour to meet you, more like!' Lorna gushed. 'I've been dreaming of this for months. Years, even. I've been a fan since the very first series.'

Amy prayed her sister wouldn't curtsy.

'Harry is already coveting your car.'

She found herself trying to defuse her colleagues' fan worship.

Mal turned to Harry and grinned. 'It's a bit of a beast but you're welcome to inspect it.' He proffered keys. 'Feel free to sit behind the wheel.'

'Muddy boots. Maybe another time.' But Harry's face glowed at the offer, and Amy guessed Mal had already sailed through the introduction test.

Mal walked through their barn-style open plan café, nodding and acting like an experienced pilot about to embark on a challenging flight.

Trepidation curled inside her. Would this be an easy journey? Or turbulent air currents?

'The website doesn't do this justice. I love the height of the place. And the styling.'

Amy liked what he'd told them so far, even though — as the website designer — his comment jarred. But at least he was being constructive and he'd taken note.

Hopefully this man wasn't ego over substance. But maybe this was a charm offensive and she shouldn't be so easily sold over?

Amy asked, 'Does that mean our website needs work?' She hoped this wasn't the case. Especially as the website was her weekly task and she'd really tried to make it stand out in design terms.

Mal shook his head.

'I mean it's bigger than it appeared. The views are more stunning. And there are more fairylights than I'd anticipated. Quite the show! You ladies like to twinkle.'

Amy felt herself blush. 'That's my sister. She can't be stopped, Believe me, I've tried. Every time I take a set down, another new one appears. Be grateful it's not worse as I had a cull a few weeks back.'

'As a matter of fact I like it. It must look great at dusk!' Mal grinned and flashed white teeth. Then he watched her, from under dark lashes so curly they were criminal on a man. His direct gaze verged on piercing and upped her pulse rate.

'It has a great atmosphere. So don't panic — we've plenty to investigate before I'm qualified to recommend. Can we sit and chat today? The process is really just about get-to-know-yous at this stage.'

Mal stood back and smiled warmly at them.

'Come on — let's sit down and talk

properly,' Lorna encouraged.

They guided Mal to the back of the café and Amy gathered drinks requests, then handed them to Josie, their waitress. She might be playing it cool but Amy could see that underneath the girl bubbled with the thrill of having a VIP guest. She hoped Josie's hands wouldn't wobble with their order.

Today their catering assistant Rex was covering for Lorna's break. He was a great kid, but Amy hoped hard he wouldn't get nervous and start dropping crockery again.

Mal sat down and swiftly got down to business.

'For starters — please don't think I'm the café inspector who will start criticising everything and making this awkward. I'm on your side. I'm here to help,' he told them.

It felt as if he'd read her mind. Of course it felt like having an inspector come to call.

He was talented. And his job was to come in and trouble-shoot. Look for areas that needed improvement. That was the point of their contest win. Who wouldn't be intimidated by that? Especially when this place was the embodiment of all their hard work and input. She remembered their humble origins too well, and she felt as if the business was her baby.

Lorna's exclamation was louder than the coffee machine on full steam.

'Hallelujah, Mal! I'm so glad you said that. About not feeling inspected. That's a huge relief.'

Mal went on, 'Any ideas I have are my opinion only. It's subjective. You don't have to agree or take them on.'

Amy noticed her sister's fingers shaking as she placed them on the waxed wooden table.

He smiled. 'Believe it or not I've been looking forward to this assignment,' he confided. 'And getting to know Derbyshire again. I used to visit as a boy — my aunt and uncle lived here. You're in a beautiful spot. So let's get down to business, make a draft timeline, and pencil in some dates. I promise I'll try to make this as painless as possible,' he asserted.

They all hoped he could set them on the right path via his agreed two months' mentoring. Amy hoped it wasn't all smooth talk and conjecture. She didn't think she could handle if this famous business mentor came in and ripped the place apart at the seams. She really hoped he would be constructive, helpful . . . but mainly kind.

Their drinks arrived complete with a tray of bakes and gourmet sandwich fingers, as previously organised by Lorna.

Amy decided to change the topic in order to deflect from her own misgivings.

'Sounds great! But first, please eat and keep my sister happy. She's been planning that finger food for days. It's not every day we get someone like you come to sample our wares.'

Mal picked up a sandwich, inspected it and then grinned. 'You don't have to ask twice. And you've done your homework on my favourites. Now I know I'm going to like it here.'

Amy still had to push through and show willing, and try not to dwell on her real view that Mal Donaldson may only be here as a career publicity stunt to suit his own aims. Would their contest win really yield results?

She was a realist. She also didn't believe that any help came free of charge. Or without underlying motives.

She'd love to think otherwise but sadly the past had taught her a hard lesson. There was usually no such thing as a free lunch. Everyone had an underlying agenda.

She knew this because she'd experienced Mal's smooth and charming type before. And she'd been spat out afterwards and left reeling.

Amy had a nagging, leaden doubt on her shoulder that unfortunately their business angel might not prove to be what Lorna hoped for at all.

★   ★   ★

A plane took off noisily outside the café's glass wall and Mal was transported back years, as if he'd stepped from a time-machine.

He walked over to observe its ascent and trailed it with his eyes. As a boy he remembered how his father loved planes, airports and watching the jets lined up on the tarmac. He'd had enough practice in his own jet-set career, even though his parents were no longer here. They'd never have guessed he'd be so widely travelled in adulthood. They'd both have coveted such a life; travel being their biggest love and hobby.

Unfortunately it had also led to their shock demise. Taken aback at his train of thought, Mal steered away from the dark feelings; shocked at what the sight of a few vintage planes could conjure up.

'This is a room with a view,' he remarked.

This place, on the very edge of High Marsh Meadow Aerodrome near Bakewell filled him with the mounting excitement he'd felt as a boy. It almost took his breath away. And these days that was rare.

The Hideaway Café was a rustic haven that had already endeared itself to him. He could see easily why the place was such a hit, and the airfield was the cherry on the cake. He envied their small, niche nook with a million-dollar view of the sky.

It felt strange being back in Britain at all, but most especially in Derbyshire where his interest in food had been born. Prior to his most recent assignments, he'd skulked at his place in France for a year. Evading the press. Avoiding his present.

Now it felt as if he'd just walked into a dream from his past.

And he wasn't sure how he felt about that. Glad? Surprised? Or just guilty?

The airfield was so close you could almost touch the planes — as if they were on a TV screen made real.

He spoke again. 'Many of these are vintage planes.'

Lorna answered, 'Yes. It's a vintage air museum. We benefit from the tourist visitors. The museum's tiny tea room shut after it ran out of volunteers. We fell for the setting and took a leap of faith; built the place to be rustic and small. Our dad used to bring us here as children.'

Amy added, 'It's also a small-scale working aerodrome.'

'What made you do this?' he quizzed.

Amy told him, 'We promised to use our inheritance wisely and do what we loved. Lorna ran a city centre sandwich bar but it was long hours for low pay, and I was an art tutor. We broke free, bought two caravans to live in and built it bit by bit.'

Mal remarked, 'Pretty brave. And extreme.'

'That's a polite way of saying crazy. It felt pretty scary and mad at the time but now it's well worth all the cold days we slogged with no hot shower at the end of a long shift.'

The vast mural on the café's main wall was another of its charms — all sky and clouds, birds, crazy flying beasts and the odd air balloon. In the far corner even a cherub perched atop a cloud. This was bold, quirky, almost graffiti. The sky outside was watchable but this one inside inspired as a feast for the soul and the eyes.

'Who painted all this?' he asked, sipping his very decent coffee and recognising that High Marsh Hideaway wasn't just any old café. For coffee and escapism both. No wonder they'd won the Fledgling Business Breakthrough contest hands down.

Lorna said, 'Amy did it. She isn't just full of backchat and attitude. She has some skills.'

He was glad to have time to chat to Lorna without Amy listening in and getting defensive. She was over in the kitchen talking to the staff — he tried to steer his own attention away and failed, yet again. He sensed she liked to deflect attention from herself onto others, and hide out of sight.

'It's stunning.' He was no art buff,

but being a chef he still liked to think he had an eye for great visual impact. This woman could conjure it in spades. He looked around to congratulate her but she'd gone.

Lorna came to stand beside him before the mural. 'She's always been multimedia. She often paints. Then she crafts and does textiles, sometimes pottery. But she also loves to do other things. Dad used to call her a dabbler. And we guessed that's why she finally plumped for public art tutoring and then wanted to come here and let creativity loose. She's a brilliant tutor — it's part of the reason I think maximising this place as an educational venue and workshop space is so vital. She really could make this place a landmark.'

Dabbler? Magician? Art genius?

Why wasn't this woman's work in some London gallery earning her a huge following and praise?

'She's quite a talent. You did this?' He directed the comment at Amy, who had just re-entered the room.

He saw her shyness and reticence, evident in her heightened complexion, but decided to go there anyway. The fact she began to look so uncomfortable reined him in.

'My way of avoiding a proper job,' she answered defensively.

'If that's not a proper job, I don't want one,' Mal answered.

Lorna explained, 'The café and the art part of the business are equal billing in profit terms. But it's Harry's veg shop that gets the customers in daily and is the real breadwinner. We don't compete generally. We're just doing our own things.'

This was so not what he'd expected when he'd got behind the wheel this morning. Sure, he'd seen the website. Perused it at length, impressive in a low-budget manner. But it did the place no justice.

And what he'd thought would amount to a case of passing on a few token menu-building tips and business expansion suggestions suddenly didn't fit the case. This deserved more than that.

This was something. Different. Unique. Special.

And that was before they broke free and expanded as they wished to.

And yet he was aware of the tricky side to this project. The rustic, shabby, fairytale make-and-mend style may well have to be streamlined. Would expanding erase the charm? They'd have to take care.

He tried to make eye contact with Amy but failed because she didn't readily engage that way.

'I can see why you want to develop the potential as an events and education venue. It's ripe for it. I see you've already tried to make it like a gallery.'

'We hope by expanding to encourage lets. Educational input. We already work with a local school in a small, informal way. But there are opportunities for so much more in educational terms. We want to make it a hub.'

Yet he wasn't sure whether he was so transfixed by the place, or the unexpectedness of the woman in his path.

He was keen to dig deeper.

'So how long does it take to create a mural like this?'

'Oh. Never ask an artist that. How long is a bit of string?' She shrugged.

'Ballpark figure, then?'

'Well . . . to actually paint, one week. Two weeks if there are issues. But it's the planning stage that takes build-up. Sometimes there are glitches. Or artist's block.'

He sensed she wanted him there, yet didn't. He sensed someone confident in her own skin and abilities, yet totally scared of others. Introvert and enigma both.

Amy Chambers had mid-brown hair in natural curls. *Crazy curls*, as his aunt had called them, because she'd had them too.

So why were his thoughts swerving off to areas like Amy's hair?

Maybe he'd been watching her strangely in silence because Amy felt obliged to speak.

'So, Mal. You think you can help us

get to the next level?'

'Absolutely. I'm positive.'

He'd had a full tour and a rundown of their strengths; their weaknesses and proposed aims he'd identified already. He'd given them homework for working out their wish-lists the next time they met.

He answered, 'I see no reason for you not to achieve your objectives. I like what you've done so far in terms of opening out the space. I'm pretty sure we can help with more construction work and a tailored plan to get this in place in the minimum timescale.'

'Great. But I don't want to rush and have regrets later.'

He felt that oddly negative vibe again.

'I hope you won't. You'll have full sanction all the way.'

Her sister stepped forward, bringing a plate of delicious-smelling pastries.

'I think I've eaten enough already, Lorna,' he protested.

He sensed one sister was worried

about the other and was here to check up on her. Lorna proved him right when she told him, 'To say we're excited and overwhelmed is an understatement. We can't wait to get started.'

'Please don't hero-worship just because of my reputation. I'm nothing special, just a working class lad done good, thanks to hard work and a lot of luck. I'm here to help. The business angel thing is short for somebody with a bit more experience, and contacts to help you get what you want. I'm plain old Mal. I want you to spend the next week thinking of your priorities, your worries, your hopes. I need to know these things. Let's not stand on ceremony and instead, let's get to the guts of things.'

He noticed the look the women shared. He couldn't read what it said and wished he could decipher.

'So which sister is the boss?' he asked. It was a joke he hoped to pull Amy's leg with. Yet he'd no idea if she'd see it that way.

Lorna pointed at Amy. 'She's younger.

But definitely the bossy boots.'

Amy faked shock. 'She means I'm the boring, sensible one. Lorna's a bit more crazy and loud; more exhibitionist than I'd like. But her vegan chilli nachos are legend, and most of our repeat customers come for those and our cakes. She's a talented woman, and a total foodie through and through.'

'And you are the sanity?'

'I try to be. I'm mostly in the workshop and shop. And in commissions for public art. We take some students from the local special education unit for art therapy and I'm really hoping to expand that. A lot of what I do is art, but I also do the business admin — I believe in being organised.'

'And you're expanding into workshops and short courses?'

'Until now it's been ad-hoc. Getting a permanent facility and education space will take extra permanent staff. But we think there's demand, and a recent pilot showed promise.'

'It's a great idea. And whose idea was

the social element of your work?'

He saw Lorna nod to her sister again. But when Amy didn't respond she did for her.

'Amy used to work with a homelessness project in London. She has links for homeless volunteers to come and work for bed, board and training. So far we've trained up catering assistants and gardeners. A veg box scheme organiser loved it so much he's stayed. And that's before Amy tells you about the art trainees she's looking to mentor.'

Mal looked to Amy but she didn't elaborate. Her frame was swamped in an oversized shirt, jeans and a sackcloth apron. You'd never guess she was a social enterprise whizz as well as an artist who could earn a fortune if she so wished.

Why did she hide?

She surprised him by softly admitting, 'I used to volunteer in a shelter and helped out over Christmas. I couldn't walk away afterwards. Now we offer short-term placements to train homeless people who want skills. They come for a bed and board arrangement and they work where their skills fit best. We initially see how we all gel before they commit themselves.'

Mal admitted, 'And it's the main reason you won the contest for funding and mentoring. It's inspiring.'

And he wondered how a woman could do such amazing things and act as if they weren't much at all.

Lorna interjected, 'You'll meet our team next visit. They'll be over the moon. It's not every day a business like ours gets such a boost. Seriously, Mal. I'm such a fan. Will you sign the books I have?'

'Of course.'

As he turned to do so, Amy surprised him.

'We never expected to win. We didn't even anticipate being selected, never mind going through heats to the final. What's in it for you?'

Mal realised something about the woman stirred him. The way she rushed out what she said or thought hard before answering, while Lorna openly bubbled like an energetic brook.

'Simple. I'm escaping the rat race. Taking time out of the public eye. And as quirky escapes go — this place is the full deal. I may have a successful career but even famous chefs can go through messy home lives. Mine was a very public breakup that impacted on my business. So I'm up for a fresh start.'

He wanted this. He really hoped their ideas would fly. He figured he could help them because he was ready to work again.

'I'll take your figures away and aim for a team meeting when I'm back,' he said. He had a good feeling about High Marsh Hideaway. He was pretty much already hooked in and rooting for them to succeed. 'We're going to do this. Trust in it.'

After several years of everything being wrong on a massive scale in his own life, Mal believed in following gut instinct and holding on with resolute belief.

2

Amy's friend and colleague had a voice that carried when she was excited. Josie almost screamed the words.

'I can't wait to meet him properly! Is he as lovely as he looks on his show?'

'Calm down, Jose! You're as bad as Lorna. You should hear her. She's got him signing her bookshelf contents now. I had to come out to the veg patch to escape. She's acting insane. How's the art store stocktake going?'

'It's doing fine. Nearly finished. How can you talk about work when we've a celeb in our midst? And a gorgeous one too.'

Josie was their first Hideaway volunteer and had stayed on since. They'd first become firm friends and confidantes at the homeless project. And it was pretty humbling to hear Josie's stories of years spent living rough.

She grinned as she confided, 'When I was selling The Big Issue Mal Donaldson had an article inside. I tore out the pictures in two copies but sold them anyway. I felt really bad but I kept it because I figured a man who looked that good must smell really amazing too! Whoever would have thought one day me and him would be working in the same place?'

The excitement in Josie's voice told Amy that Lorna wasn't the only fan in the building.

'You're welcome to him, Jose. He's too clean cut for me. I like a man with a bit of paint on his hands or mud on his boots.'

'Liar. That last guy of yours, Jason, wasn't remotely like that and you fell for him big time. He was all slick clothes and hipster beard.'

And she had all the scars to prove her bad choice. She didn't want reminding of the guy who'd dropped her from a height so hard she'd almost snapped in two. In fact, he was the reason she'd left

London. And in coming here she'd aimed to leave him behind; not have him tagging her years after.

Only he wouldn't . . . because he'd moved on and he'd broken her heart.

'Can we just not go there?'

'He was a restaurant owner and you fancied him, that's all I meant. Shame you did really. He was a right chancer.' Amy could hear regret in her friend's voice. 'Sorry, Amy. I didn't mean to poke at old wounds.'

'Why does everyone feel the need to get involved in my life and give me advice?' Amy's sharp words made Josie scowl.

'Sorry. I didn't mean to sound mean.'

'I know you didn't. And you haven't offended me. Ooops. I can see Mal and Lorna coming out — better go. Are we on for Friday night? A proper catch-up?'

'Absolutely. And I want all the gossip, including insider insights. I especially need you to tell me just how good he smells in the flesh. Call it something I just need to know.'

Amy sighed deeply but held back a smile as she went to meet her mentor, imagining what he'd say if she greeted him with a sniff.

*   *   *

The figures stood up. As the business brain as well as the creative force at High Marsh Hideaway Amy knew her figures back to front.

Mal scrutinised her screen and questioned her. His scent was shower-fresh citrus. She figured she'd keep that knowledge to herself rather than admit it to Josie.

'So these are projections for when you open up for evening trade? And the figures for the art workshops and additional leases?'

'Yes. They're all there. Business plan. Full case history from our start-up too.'

'And these are your accounts for last year?'

'Last three years. Full details. I don't

think anything's been missed.'

She felt herself bristle when he put on thick trendy tortoiseshell spectacles from a case in his jacket pocket as if he was about to swoop. 'Profit and loss for all areas? What about bank details, payroll?'

'I'm not trying to hide anything from you.' She felt her eyelid tic start up.

Mal stared up at her and she saw him stop before he said something. Then he paused.

'I'd never dream of suggesting that. Do I take it you're finding my presence intrusive?' His gaze zoned in on hers and stayed there. Then he flipped off the spectacles. They suited him way too well. Smart. Sexy. Well-groomed designer guy.

Amy admitted, 'No. I'm just not used to being questioned.'

'I'm only checking I have what I need. I don't intend having any issue with any of it. Just saving myself a job later and stopping me from pestering you further down the line.' He put his specs away. 'If we have a problem then I think we should deal with that now, don't you?'

Mal laid down his folder of papers, sat on the desk edge and fixed her with a stare.

Amy wanted to run. She hated conflict. And the last thing she wanted to do was admit her inner gripes right now, on day one. She'd far rather wait and see the lie of the land before she vented.

Mal was quicker than she was ready for.

'So you aren't as keen on this as your sister? That's pretty plain for me to read. What I can't work out is, why? You're clearly an originating force behind the whole place, so why feel so threatened?'

'It's not that.'

'What is it, then? Because clearly you're more reserved. And perhaps you're finding relinquishing the tight hold you have on the business harder than you can admit. And before you deny that I'd just like to say, that's OK. I'd be exactly the same if somebody came into one of my restaurants. The part you're forgetting is that I really am on your side here. I just need a background knowledge so I'm up to speed super-fast. We need to hit the ground running.'

Amy admitted, 'I've put together everything I thought you may need. But I'm more than happy for you to contact me if anything's been overlooked.'

Mal drew closer and his gaze bored into hers. 'That wasn't what I asked, Amy. Do you or don't you have a problem? With me?'

'No. I'm just more reserved than Lorna.'

'I'm not convinced that's it.'

Amy blinked at him. 'I don't want to feel this project is running away too fast. I want full control over things. I want considered decisions. We've worked too hard to let the expansion go in a wrong direction now.'

She saw his jaw twitch. 'That's the

last thing I'd want. If you're uncomfortable with anything then we stop. I can promise you that.'

'I'm glad to hear it.'

'I'm really not as bad as some of the papers make out. You know, they make up lies and rumours sometimes. I'm not the party boy. One of the articles was such a shock I almost dropped my pipe and slippers and tripped over my walking stick! Not to mention the dent it made in my ear trumpet!' Mal grinned at her. Amy found herself watching him oddly then laughing lightly.

'Wow. Now I'm really getting a picture of you I didn't expect!'

'There. The ice just broke.' Mal shoved out a hand and Amy grasped it.

Amy teased back, 'You reckon? I think you're just trying to kid me.'

Mal laughed openly. 'Amy. I'm going to make it my mission to prove to you I'm not as scary as you might think. I started out on the bottom rung, you know. It wasn't all an easy ride to fame.'

He stood up. She could smell the paper in her accounting ledgers. It felt odd handing them over to a stranger.

'I didn't say you were scary. I just think this is new ground for me.'

He nodded and sniffed. 'Give me a few weeks and I'll prove I'm worth trusting.'

'We'll see then, won't we?'

Were his antics words over substance? She'd had a relationship with a man who said all the right things and acted like the perfect host. But he only did what suited him.

Jason had been skilled in charm and proved himself deft at achieving his own aims and desires at the expense of others. She'd almost lost her direction as a result. In fact, she'd changed her life at that particular awkward crossroads.

He'd left her with little choice but to escape him.

Amy saw Mal's jaw flex as he collected the files. She realised she was holding her spine ramrod straight and her hands were fisted. She really needed to ease up.

So, yes. She had her reasons for finding Mal Donaldson thumbing through her spreadsheets and making drastic suggestions tricky. Even during the tour of her workshop and the café's outer rooms she'd suddenly felt as if someone had demoted her. That was all in her own head. Yet their small idyll definitely felt scrutinised — and that made her defensive.

Ridiculous, but true.

She wasn't used to having someone to answer to in her workspace. His voice, with its lick of northern accent, affected her. She heard every word, even when she tried not to. It felt as if they'd had a new surprise guest to stay, and she hadn't prepped and had to be on best behaviour.

But she'd vowed to give him time. To go with this and reserve judgment for now.

She tried to sum up and encourage him to end the conversation.

'You'll have all you need in this project file. The spreadsheets with all the figures are appended. I'm here and willing to answer any questions you have. Is that all?'

'I think so. I'll get back soon. The main requirement will be finessing the expansion. It's a big step from a café to forty covers, and an education centre over the odd training session.'

'We don't take it lightly. And we wouldn't try if we didn't think we were capable.'

'I have full faith in all of your ideas and abilities.' He reached out to touch her arm and Amy felt herself draw back on reflex.

The phone rang on the desk and Mal moved away so that Amy could pick it up.

One of Amy's extra-curricular pursuits was to act as a befriender to a local girl with extra support needs. It was her mother, Kathy Craig, checking pick-up times.

'I'm afraid Phoebe's been challenging

this week,' Kathy confided. 'I thought it was only fair to warn you, Amy.'

'It can't be easy having month-old triplets at home. She's always good when she comes to the Hideaway. Though I try to keep her focused and busy. I don't let her act up, either.'

'She's readjusting. We'll get there. Having you step in a few times a week is great for her. I thought it best to mention her behaviour in case there's any minor blow-ups.'

'I look forward to seeing her tonight after school. Your warning is much appreciated, Kathy.'

Amy brought her attention back to the here and now. She took stock and recognised her own state. Maybe, like Phoebe, she too was struggling with the flux. Perhaps she should focus on the opportunity and do this anyway. She drew in a breath. Easier to say than do.

This was like getting your first mortgage, but worse. She still had issues with risk. Old habits had left her smarting.

'Please be assured I've no issue with

you being here, Mal.'

'I'm glad. And I hope to get back to you with productive news.'

She watched him disappear. It didn't take long for her sister to sweep back via the door he'd gone through.

Lorna's fruity, spicy perfume was as vibrant as she was and it dispelled the lingering aroma of Mal. She remarked, 'He's taking love-struck car freak to view the dream machine. I think Harry may never recover. He's even changed his boots and trousers so he can go for a spin. What's up? You've been quiet . . . '

'It feels weird having to answer to someone else, that's all.'

'It was you who entered the competition.'

Amy shrugged, and tried to brush off the negative feelings she couldn't explain.

'Don't you like him?'

'I just find letting go of the reins hard,' Amy admitted.

'Hardly a surprise after slimeball Jason, the rip-off merchant, used you so badly. Come through before he goes.

What you're feeling is entirely natural. But I'm not going to let Mal Donaldson ever be a user like Jason Hynd was. I'll dent his bumpers before I'd let him do that.'

Amy closed her computer down. Why did she feel such a fool acting this way? Answer — she knew why. The tiny box of heartbreak had been hidden so deep she had hoped to avoid ever confronting the issues again.

Jason's wounds still cut her deep. She just didn't want to admit it. Even to herself.

★   ★   ★

Lorna had served grilled veggie wraps with all the famous Hideaway salad trimmings as a conclusion to Mal's tour. He'd eaten it as if ravenous. Amy was shocked, given that he'd already been stuffed with finger sandwiches and pastries; his appetite was fierce.

He must have felt the need to explain. 'I drove for hours this morning and couldn't cram in breakfast. Sorry. This is too good to resist.'

Her sister kidded him. 'Such a confession from a lauded chef — that's scandalous.'

'I'm quite glad I waited. It means I can eat more here. It's delicious.'

Didn't celebrity chefs make snack breaks a priority? He'd even raved about their home-grown salad with edible flower garnish and asked for Lorna's ingredient details.

Amy guessed he was just trying hard to make friends. Lorna was easily won. Which was just as well given her own reticence.

'The more I see the more I love,' he'd gushed before he left. 'I'll be back to you all soon. Count on it. First I have to go and find lodgings in Derbyshire for when I'm here. I have the address of a hotel with an annexe in Matlock. Sounds ideal but we'll have to see.'

'We have a small spare room in our barn studios. Why not stay here?'

Lorna's offer was out before even Amy

could stop her. And again Amy wished her sister would check first. Mal kept his gaze away, but the sisters exchanged sharp glances that didn't need words.

Mal answered swiftly, 'That's kind, but I think it's best if I give you space. Right. I'll be off. Don't worry, I'll see Harry on my way out. We'll speak again soon.'

Amy immediately felt a sharp rush of guilt at the bad vibes assault. Now the man would think she was opposed to him. She could already see the disappointment in Lorna's taut expression and feel her irritation.

She wished she really was as confident as she pretended. Or comfortable with direct praise. Or criticism.

She glimpsed her reflection in the café's glass mirror; she looked drained. Maybe her introversion was too challenged when it came to a certain successful Yorkshire chef. He of the chiselled jawline, dark hair, easy charm, good looks and business genius.

Amy felt herself roughly pulled from

her thoughts into her sister's insistent orbit when the words yanked her from her thoughts.

'What's up with you? You said be confident — *act like we can do it* was your mantra. And now you've turned all quiet and grumpy. If you scare him off you'll never live it down.'

Amy blew out a breath. 'Sorry. I'll try harder.'

'Bit late to think that now. Nice first impression you made.'

She'd disappointed her sister. Not just the boyfriend who'd always wanted her to do better, used her to promote his own aims, then found someone better suited for the long haul. He'd made her put her guard up so fully, now she'd messed up with their VIP business angel.

'I'm sorry, sis. Truly. I'll do better next time.'

Amy knew she'd just been guilty of acting as if all men were massive manipulators.

Jason Hynd was in the past. Was she really still that bitter?

She'd done Mal a disservice. She'd have to do better. Providing she hadn't screwed up irreparably already.

★ ★ ★

The scent of damp grass brought back unbidden memories of long childhood days, and summers spent grazing knees in bike stunts gone wrong.

The pub was overgrown and rambling, creepers hung from its guttering and wood barred the windows and door.

Even now in his mind's eye Mal remembered the shiny red door and brass door fittings. And his aunt polishing like she tended the brass of her beloved bar fixtures — gleaming like jewels in her crown. Their pub had been their world. Their child — until he'd come along and then they'd opened that world up to him without question.

An orphan — clinging to his tiny baby sister because she was all he had left. Two young lives whose worlds had caved in.

Yet his aunt and uncle had turned him from a quiet, shell-shocked boy into a kid with potential, skills, flair and eventually a talent worthy of sharing. He'd started out doing odd jobs for his uncle then eventually proved his talent in the kitchen and been promoted to Kitchen Hand.

The chef part had been a natural step.

Mal stood outside with the agent, having just removed the For Sale sign.

The dark windows of the pub felt like dismayed eyes staring at him accusingly. Voicing their profound disappointment that he should ever have tried to be rid of his past.

'It's a shame it didn't sell,' the agent said. 'We did have interest. But unfortunately you deemed the offers unsuitable.'

'I wanted more for this place than flats. And a fast food chain was out of the question.'

He itched to leave — at speed — and jangled the car keys in his hand. Sensory overload. Memory Lane had become a place of pain.

'It would have made you a lot of money, Mr Donaldson. Re-enlivened the local area. Ever consider that? Now it's still an eyesore.'

'Well. Sometimes fate makes you face things. I can turn this around my way. It could be a great restaurant again with the right attention. It should reflect its past.'

How long ago those carefree summer days felt now. Especially looking at the sight before him. His uncle's place; his mentor had long gone. The man who'd led him into his vocation. Who'd turned him into a real working chef with all the skills at a young age. *RIP Patrick Donaldson.*

Mal kept tight rein on his emotions. He didn't let the enormity overwhelm him.

He'd promised to return to see him but hadn't made it in time. If he'd realised just how sick Uncle Paddy was, he'd have returned in a blink. He should have prioritised better, and realised he needed more care after his aunt had passed. But then he figured the old man hadn't wanted him to know how sick he was.

I'm back now, Uncle Paddy, he said softly in his head. *Too late. I'm sorry I wasn't here. And I regret that I tried to walk away.*

He turned to go, saying over his shoulder to the agent, 'So that's it off the market?'

'Yes. I have some last documents to sign.'

'Could you email them?'

The woman's voice clawed at his peace of mind. 'Can't we do it now, since you're here? You were very hard to get hold of before.'

Derbyshire. He should have gone with instinct and voted against the Hideaway project for personal reasons alone. But he wasn't that shallow. His own history couldn't stand in the way of the best project on the table . . . and the fact he'd evaded his inheritance until this point.

The agent — Sally — who'd initially asked for autographs and a selfie on her phone was now all clipped and business-like.

'Even though the place is rather run-down, it has a lot of potential. You should open it up as your own place. People would flock here with your name on the sign.'

'We'll see. No definite plans.'

He couldn't have lived with himself if he'd given The Hideaway a no vote just because he'd long delayed dealing with this inheritance. He could no longer live with his deep denial about his uncle's stagnating pub.

Mal had flowers in the car. Roses for his aunt for the cemetery; he'd briefly go there next. For Paddy, there were geraniums like the ones he'd grown in hanging baskets outside the pub.

Mal vowed this had to be a turning point. He had to put this right. He was no stranger to hard graft. He'd spent way too long mourning the past; that was never going to change anything.

★　★　★

Only thirty seconds after the second bell rang, Phoebe torpedoed into Amy's arms. Her blonde hair flew in the breeze and curled around her cheeks. She'd most likely hate the curls when she was older, as much as Amy did her own.

Phoebe accosted her with enthusiastic questions and statements, an energetic buzz on legs that didn't stop for breath. No wonder her mother appreciated the respite. But wasn't that part of her young charge's charm?

'Hey! Amy. We made hedgehogs from clay in art. I want to give you one of them.'

'Sounds amazing. Can't wait to see. But maybe you should keep it for your mum.'

'I want to give it to you — Mum won't mind. Mine had enormous glow in the dark eyes that made me and Tyler laugh until we nearly fell over. Then we learned all the French colours and found out which fruit floats or sinks but had to work it all out by talking in French.

Which was a bit crazy. And tomorrow's practising for country dancing. We're going in for a competition —'

Phoebe really needed to calm down — or come with ear defenders and headache pills. Which was one of the reasons Amy was so needed in this role as this child's befriender.

'Phoebe! Time to take a breath. One sentence at a time, or I can't keep up. And that would be a shame because I love your stories. I just like to hear and understand them all properly.'

Phoebe handed her the violin case and a bag of who knows what. 'But did you even know that grapes sink, Amy? Apples float and grapes sink. Did you know?'

No, she didn't know. Nor much about other fruit's floating capabilities.

'Crazy,' she answered. 'Life's full of strange stuff sometimes.'

She'd learned a great deal since taking up a role at the Befriending Service for kids with additional needs. She'd also learned new things about herself. For instance, that sometimes her reservations made her appear offputting and put her at risk of offending the amazing mentor they'd been lucky enough to be awarded. Yes — big lessons learned, even in adult life.

She'd also noticed that Mal Donaldson had amazing caramel glints in his chocolate-brown eyes. She'd tried not to notice. Or to stare. And when he wore his glasses, it magnified them. She'd found it hard to hold eye contact, too — that was really too pathetic to be true. If she admitted it to her sister or Josie they'd tease her for weeks.

She'd never admit it to anyone but Mal had eyes like those of puppies that stole your heart. He was dangerous because he was very gorgeous. And hideously talented. And much as she wanted to disapprove of him, he had blown her away with some of his off-the-cuff suggestions. His full recommendations would be awesome.

But would he really see it through to completion?

'What's for tea at the café tonight, Amy? Say it's lasagne, please, please, you know it's my favourite. With crunchy edges and garlic bread.'

'As it happens, there's homemade pizza on the menu tonight. Do you fancy that, if I persuade them to add garlic bread?'

'Yes! Pizza is yum too!'

They walked from the playground towards the car. In the short time Amy had been working with Phoebe, just under a year, her ADHD was already noticeably improving thanks to a combination of medication and thera-pies. The after-school one-to-one art therapy Amy offered her was, her mum told her, a Godsend. Amy honestly enjoyed the challenge of encouraging and helping the ten-year-old to focus and develop her interests and strengths.

'Were you busy at work, Amy? You seem tired.'

'I was busy today. But never too tired to do creative art with you. I have modelling clay. What do you want to make? I thought we might make vases and keep it a secret as a gift for your Mum.'

Her grin was elfin. 'More hedge-hogs?'

'If hedgehog is what you most want . . . how about a vase with a hedgehog theme?'

'Yay! Race you to the car.'

'In these boots?' Amy pointed to her heels. Normally she wore her walking boots but she had tried to look smarter today. And it annoyed her that having Mal Donaldson visiting had made her feel the need to act differently.

Phoebe teased in a sing-song voice, 'You're just making excuses. Three, two, one.'

Amy set off sprinting as Phoebe's laughter echoed — reminding her of someone else who'd already laughed at her that day.

3

The smell of rich roast beef gravy lingered and Mal felt guilty, knowing that his new vegan business acquaintances may not approve.

He pushed away his plate, then blinked in surprise. Eating every bite was unusual, given his super-high standards, but he'd been happy to wipe out his entire portion tonight.

The Old Mill did a mean roast dinner and a full-on day had left him famished. To think he'd devoured all Lorna Chambers' food too!

'You enjoyed your meal?' Mrs Milton asked, her Derbyshire accent as welcoming as a warm, soft blanket. Her eyes twinkled at him. Why was it that, being a chef, everyone craved your culinary compliments? And tried to stuff you to maximum capacity? He was going to get fat if he wasn't careful.

'Delicious. You'll see the only thing I left was the pattern on the plate.'

Mrs Milton grinned. 'That's what I was hoping for! And I've no problem having a loose arrangement with meals. Just give me notice in the morning if you want me to prepare you something. Or text me if something comes up. I'm not great with texts but our Benny keeps me right.'

Mal smiled. 'I couldn't ask for better. All that hospitality and a gorgeous room. I've lucked out! To think the last place I stayed was a beach hut in Phuket with a resident spider. Very glad to be back. And spider-free.'

'We're glad to have you.' Mrs Milton smiled as she tidied away the dishes. 'Would you like coffee, something sweet? I have some crumble.'

Mal shook his head. He was fortunate to have booked the annexe to the main hotel for privacy. Being a known face had advantages and pitfalls. She'd offered to deliver his meals to the lodge. This way he could look around, at his pace. Get a better feel for the place. Fathom plans.

His phone rang. Sheila, his agent, was instantly recognisable thanks to her Texan accent.

'Tell me you'll make Friday's breakfast show? Or have you crawled into a hole, joined a monastery, or taken up some strange Durr-bee-shire habit? Please don't say it's Morris dancing or I'll know you've lost the plot.'

Mal rolled his eyes. 'Friday. Ingrained on my mind and my calendar. When have I ever let you down? Or danced in public, for that matter?'

'Don't get me started. You've never reneged on a job but you have kept me waiting for answers. Including you coming back to the UK.'

'TV series and books take time, Sheila.'

And the will to fulfil them.

'I meant the disappearance to France. I'd like to catch up on Friday. Lunch — I'll book?'

'Invite me to yours instead; I'll cook.'

'Really?'

'Lately I've been itching to. I can't invite you to mine as it has tenants. Right now I'm of no fixed abode, though today I've found somewhere to hang out temporarily. A hotel that exceeds five stars in my book.' He said it so Mrs Milton could overhear.

Sheila got right back to her mission.

'I intend to grill you; I have offers. Projects needing answers. I'll nail you down on your future schedule. You're still in demand.'

Why did that cause his temples to throb?

He already knew his answer. She wouldn't welcome it. He intended to continue to evade the fame with no thoughts of profile-boosting whatsoever — just personal dreams realised. He was finally striking out.

'See you Friday.'

'And just as a warning . . . that woman's been after you. Zara; she keeps calling like I'm your secretary. I handle your business affairs, not any other ones, Mal. If you want to stonewall her, don't expect me to pick up the flack. She's too full of herself for this Texan to play nice much longer.'

Mal rubbed the back of his head. 'Zara Lake. I'll deal with her. I'll put her straight yet again. If she calls you, feel free to hang up.'

'You're getting very assertive in your old age.' He heard the smile in his agent's voice.

'When was thirty-three past it?'

'You're also harder to get hold of. We need to talk about that.'

Little did she know that he was about to become impossibly hard to get hold of — on a regular basis. 'You're right. We do need to talk.'

Mal replaced the phone. Telling himself that even though Sheila may not like it, assertiveness was now his shorthand for 'making amends' and 'changed man'.

★   ★   ★

'Elgar — come back here!'

Amy's shouting was fruitless because the dog wasn't listening.

'Stop that now!' Amy ordered as Phoebe turned a series of expert cartwheels, proving her school gymnastics prowess. The dog, meanwhile, had a crazy fit doing laps round the dubious-smelling pond then rolling vigorously in a mass of something soggy that filled her with dread.

Phoebe remarked, 'He loves being outside. Just like I do.'

'If he's not careful I'll stop bringing him. He goes too mad. And I'm the one who has to bath him. It's awful when he gets in a state.'

'You can tell he's happy by the way he sniffs the air like this.' Her young charge acted like a hound sniffing a trail.

'Are you going to help me clean him up before we take you back to your mum's?'

'Do I have to go? It's so boring! Babies crying. Babies eating. They don't even play,' Phoebe protested. 'All I can do is rub their heads.'

'That's not nice or fair. Your mum's very busy since the triplets were born.'

It was one of the main reasons Phoebe's case had been referred to the befriending service for increased provision. Phoebe had issues that meant caring for her brought extras; ADHD and high-functioning autism. But her mother's three-baby surprise meant she really needed a hand at home.

Phoebe did a flip over into a crab then expertly righted herself in a move that could draw applause from an audience. All conducted with a grin and in wellies. Girl and dog both were balls of energy.

Amy noted, 'Maybe doing all those moves with a tummy full of pizza isn't wise.'

Elgar ran right up to Amy, jumping on her so that his wet paws stamped patterns on her jeans. Phoebe laughed as if it was the funniest thing she'd seen in weeks.

Amy chastised the dog. 'If you don't stop I'm going to confiscate your favourite toy!'

'Are you always this rowdy and commanding on walks?' a voice asked. 'Can't a tourist get any peace around here?'

Amy started and whirled. She hadn't heard anyone approach and found her heart was already racing hard and the panic reflex had kicked in proper. She hadn't expected to be accosted by unexpected strangers, obviously.

Only the figure was no stranger.

Mal Donaldson smiled at them. He wore jeans and a striped grey and navy sweatshirt, with a light jacket on top. He looked ready to sail a yacht. Only his boots were sensible walking ones and his hair blew in the breeze as his smile reassured her. Today he wore his glasses.

'Sorry. Didn't mean to intrude or startle you.'

'You're still here?' Amy said, then cursed her lack of guile or diplomacy.

She'd made it sound as if she wanted him as far over the county line as she could get him.

'Found a place to rent. Decided to stay around. Nice dog — hey, boy,' he called to Elgar who immediately rushed over to smother him in attention. 'What's his name?'

'Elgar. Don't make friends with him. He's terribly behaved. You'll regret it when he soaks your clothes.'

'Hey, Elgar. C'mon boy!' Mal picked up a nearby stick. Instantly the smitten dog responded.

'You won't get rid of him if you do that,' Amy warned.

'Isn't he half Tibetan Terrier, half collie?'

'You know that?'

'My uncle bred them for a while. Nice dog.'

'I'm going to have to bathe him before tea.'

Phoebe interjected, 'I'm going to stay and help. I love it when he gets bubbles on the ceiling!'

It was only then Amy realised her omission and introduced them. 'Sorry . . . you haven't met Phoebe — Mal is working with us, Phoebe.'

'Hello. I'm Mal,' he introduced. 'Great to meet you.'

Phoebe stared hard at the man beside them. 'I know you. You were in Spain on TV and cooked on the beach. And you did a crazy dance in a forest when you cooked up some kind of stew. It looked horrible.'

Amy added softly, 'Phoebe!'

A blush tinged his cheeks when he hooted with laughter. 'It wasn't one of my best. Are you a telly buff? Or just an expert on the Cookery Channel?'

'I just like eating. Lorna watches all the shows and she's really into growing food to eat.'

'I've met Lorna. I'm aiming to learn all I can from her.' Mal winked at Amy on the sly to show his current tack was a gentle tease.

Phoebe asked, 'So how do you know Amy?'

'She's teaching me about art. And people-skills,' Mal answered swiftly, then exchanged a glance with Amy. She saw his lips twitch.

His next comment surprised them both. 'I didn't know you had a daughter. Though I'm surprised I didn't guess. The energy, the hair . . . '

'Phoebe's not my daughter. She's my friend and art studio helper. She comes over to do art with me two nights a week,' Amy answered.

'Hey Phoebe, I like your curls. Did you know they are a gift from God — or at least that's what my aunt told me when she put mine into pigtails for me.' He pulled a horrified face.

'Don't be silly! Boys don't do that!' Phoebe squealed with mirth. And Amy surprised herself by laughing out loud at his open silliness.

Phoebe pushed, 'Didn't the other kids laugh?'

Mal shook his head. 'I'm kidding. I hated my curls when I was young. Now I think they are awesome. I'm helping

Amy and Lorna make the café bigger. And I was really impressed by the art. Do you like Amy's work, Phoebe?'

'She's good at pottery. People like the big sculptures. I'm more of a cartwheels girl — '

Aware Phoebe was starting to make it a one-girl-show Amy added, 'We're just heading off. If I can get this mad dog to oblige me.'

Mal whistled sharply between his teeth in a move that made them stare at each other. The dog was at his side in seconds.

'Did you really just summon my disobedient mad hairball with one whistle?'

Mal grinned. 'I have skills.'

'Clearly you do,' Amy answered softly.

Phoebe clapped her hands. 'Teach me!'

'You just have to practise, Phoebe. I'm not just a chef. Nor a dog whisperer. Nice seeing you both, I'd best get off.'

'Where are you staying?' Amy asked, now genuinely interested.

'Mill Falls Lodge. They do great dinners. Are they your closest competition?'

'They're our friends. We offer different menu styles.'

'Don't worry. I'm not defecting. I go back to London for a few days tomorrow.' He stooped to pet Elgar and the dog rolled over, tongue lolling out and showing his tummy like an easy sell.

Amy admitted, 'You have a fan.'

But she figured this man had fans lining up down the street. Now including Elgar and Phoebe.

'Bye, ladies.'

Phoebe said. 'Bye, Mister Mal. Maybe one day you'll cook us a stew in the forest?'

'Now there's an idea to keep a busy chef's brain out of trouble.' He smiled back at them.

And with that Mal Donaldson walked off, leaving Amy denying to herself that her pulse felt like a train in her veins. Questions zoomed around her head. She vowed to resist.

'I like him,' remarked Phoebe.

'You hardly know him.'

'I know his catchphrases, and that he loves to eat crusty bread and stew. And chocolate fondant. It's his trademark pudding.'

Amy boggled, realising that her young charge knew more about their Business Angel than she did herself.

'Home time soon,' she said.

Phoebe huffed out a breath. 'You're so boring, isn't she, Elgar? But we like Mr Mal. He was fun. And he likes us. Even if Amy's a party pooper.'

★   ★   ★

Phoebe kicked the car's front seat with all her might and yelled, 'No. Don't want to!'

Amy could feel it; the beginnings of a tsunami tantrum. She'd developed an instinct now.

Her pulse raced and a voice in her head begged, *Please, Phoebe — it's been a hard day.* But Phoebe's tantrums weren't something that could be switched off and on — even by her. And they just proved how much she'd accepted and felt comfortable with her befriender.

Amy breathed deeply, practising mindfulness and controlled ignoring.

Downplaying Phoebe's wilful disobedience helped. Engaging or taking a stand often made things explode. She loved the engagement which only fuelled her anger. So Amy had learned to pick battles wisely when dealing with a child who had a short fuse and reactive behavioural problems.

'We're going home now.'

'Don't want to! I want to do more clay!'

The shout was startling in its aggression.

Amy schooled herself in calm. But it was still hard. She knew if she'd behaved that way as a child she'd have been too afraid of her dad's firmness to push like that. She'd also most likely have had no supper as a consequence . . . but times had changed.

'Now! I want clay again!'

To the outsider this was a terrible ten-year-old, a brat who needed a piece of a strict parent's mind. But that was surface judgment and ignorance. For this child, the usual norms didn't fit. Phoebe couldn't self-regulate. Phoebe needed special care, treatment, time to calm down and realise she'd taken a wrong turn.

'Phoebe, you know the rules. Your mum is expecting you back soon.'

'Clay. Now. I hate you, Amy!'

She screamed so loud and whacked the car door so hard a nearby man emerging from the café to his car in the car park sent them a scowl. He stood and stared. If she'd known him she'd have struck up a defusing conversation but as she didn't, now wasn't the time to explain exactly why he should just move along.

Was she dealing with this wrong? What else should she do now?

On reflection maybe expecting a child with ADHD and autism to wait until her clay ornament had been kiln fired wasn't her cleverest move. Waiting was frustrating for everybody. But she was still learning. And beating herself up about it wouldn't help.

This was real life. Judgemental types like Mr Know Nothing could go hang with his stares.

'If you stamp and kick, then the only person you will hurt is yourself,' she said calmly.

'I hate you! Don't want to go home. I want clay. And I want crisps now!'

'We've had a lovely night together and I don't want to spoil it. Your clay will be ready on Thursday. I can't give you it when it isn't ready but I promise it will be worth it next time.'

Phoebe let out a yell, then rattled the car door handle. Thank heaven for central locking — in the mood she was proving to be in, she'd likely act out and run. If that happened she would be escalating to danger zone in a blink.

'Crisps,' she screamed. 'Crisps right now!'

In her current state there would be no breakthrough. For the sake of a bag of crisps she had to relent. There were some in the boot of her car and Amy calmly fetched them.

'You must say sorry first.'

'No.'

'No sorry, no crisps.'

'You're a meanie, Amy.'

'I'm not. But you are being mean to me. I'm your friend, and friends should always be kind to each other.'

'Sorry, then.' Phoebe took the crisps from Amy's grasp. Suddenly, from nowhere, Phoebe smiled as if a rainbow had just emerged from behind a thundercloud. 'Thank you. Sorry I had a hissy fit. I'm hungry, that's all. You are my friend really, Amy.'

Sometimes back-downs were all you had. She imagined how hard that would have been with another three baby seats in the car. Yet Amy knew she had momentarily felt like a failure. Children with extras brought challenging issues for the parents — which was exactly why she needed to continue to do this job on top of her other commitments.

The scowling man was still in his car but Amy blocked him out as she turned the key in the ignition to leave. Her silent, impotent way of getting the last word.

'We all make mistakes, Phoebe. But it's saying sorry that counts most.'

She knew how hard it was for these kids. She'd battled with ADHD and kept it hidden for years of her own life. Ultimately, it was her art that saved her. She'd found a place where she could lose herself and be herself at the same time. Without it, who knew what would have happened?

4

Mal presented his dish to the camera with a flourish and a large slice of boyish grin. So very him!

The food looked gorgeous in its own right. Some Asian fusion creation with colourful shards making it more a work of art than a delicious dinner she'd happily volunteer to eat. The women he was cooking for exclaimed over his talents and Amy, still in her pyjamas rolled her eyes at the television.

Then again, her sister would react exactly the same if Mal Donaldson had just cooked her a Thai street food wonder out of store cupboard essentials and what was left in the fridge. He went on to be judged the contest's winner by a mile.

Amy's finger hovered over the pause button but better judgment kicked in to save her. She wouldn't let herself rewind the cooking contest show just so she could stare at her new mentor. What was she even thinking?

Brushing her hair, she flicked to another channel to prevent any further crazy thoughts. What was wrong with her? She needed to get a firm grip.

Mal Donaldson was her business advisor. Period. And a celebrity. Why was she mooning about like this?

Had it been so long since she'd had a date — or noticed a handsome man, come to that — that she'd suddenly turned impressionable and daft?

She could just imagine what Lorna would say if she ever caught her ogling Mal.

Then again, Lorna was a fully subscribed Mal fan with all the gush points to prove it.

The phone rang, snatching her from her thoughts. Elgar was already running in circles awaiting his morning walk, telling her she wasn't dressing fast enough for his liking.

Her sister's name appeared on the

screen and Amy was in two minds about answering but pressed the call button anyway, risking Elgar starting barking to force her into action.

'Hi! Can we keep this brief? Elgar needs walkies and I'm not even dressed . . . '

'Amy! How fast can you get here? We need you right now! In the café!' Lorna demanded. 'It's Josie. She's collapsed. The ambulance is already coming but I thought she'd want you there with her.'

'Oh, my goodness. Coming now.'

Elgar would have to wait. Or come with her and keep himself occupied.

In just over twenty seconds Amy had a sweatshirt and joggers pulled on over her nightwear and had Elgar with her bounding over to the café at speed. Her pulse raced like a runaway dynamo and her heart was in her mouth. Amy dreaded to imagine what she was going to find when she got there.

⋆ ⋆ ⋆

Josie lay motionless on the café's rustic tiled floor. The sight made Amy's pulse hammer even harder and the shock made her blink as she struggled to formulate a plan.

Josie was more than just an employee and colleague. She was a close friend whom Amy loved like another sister, and she looked so young and vulnerable lying there limp and pale.

'What happened?' Amy asked when she reached her sister and put her hand out to touch Lorna's shoulder.

Lorna looked up her mouth trembling as she spoke. 'I was in the store cupboard and heard a bang. When I ran back in, she was on the floor. We came in early to batch cook some main meal freezer stock soup.'

'And the bang?'

'I think it was the pressure cooker, maybe? It may have been caused by plugging it in. I'm not really sure, I'm guessing — ' Lorna broke off and sobbed, the back of her hand to her mouth.

'Ambulance?' Amy tried to stall her own panic.

A knock sounded on the kitchen door, heralding paramedics arriving. Amy took charge. It was clear Lorna had had a terrible shock and needed time to recover.

The next ten minutes passed in a blur of paramedics attending to Josie who was still unresponsive. An oxygen mask was put in place as she was checked over.

Amy noticed her own hands were shaking. She felt utterly useless and traumatised.

Had their kitchen equipment been faulty and injured an employee? Would the place be condemned? Would an insurance claim follow?

Lorna's eyes were full of tears and Amy pulled her sister into a hug.

'I've no idea what happened, but that burning smell makes me think it's the pressure cooker. Which makes it our fault!' Lorna burst into fresh sobs. Amy stood holding her sister tightly, recognising that their lives had all just changed in a single moment. And not in a good way.

'It could have happened to any of us, sis.' Praying hard that Josie would be OK, Amy swallowed and tried to play the strong sister. 'One step at a time! Let's concentrate on Josie. You OK if I go with her? You want me to stay here? You're pretty pale yourself.'

'Go. I'll get Harry to come.'

'Elgar's mooching in my studio. He'll need a quick walk if Harry can manage it later.'

Lorna nodded. 'Tell me as soon as you know anything, won't you?'

'Of course, Lorna. You know I will.'

★ ★ ★

When Amy looked away from the hospital's waiting room monitor she had been staring at as if in a trance, the last person she expected to see was walking straight towards her with conviction.

'Mal! What are you doing here?'

Today he wore his glasses as if he'd just been reading and hadn't taken them off. Amy's feelings swirled like a tornado. Why did he have to turn up?

Today was panning out to be awful on an epic scale. The waiting room was full, the chairs were hard and all she really wanted to do was to urgently find out if Josie was regaining consciousness — and if not, why not.

It was bad enough, knowing nothing and sitting there imagining all the worst scenarios. Now she had Mal here to bear witness to her frayed mood and frantic worry. Now he'd think they were business failures with huge problems like dangerously faulty equipment.

'I'm here in case you need me,' he answered. 'Any news?'

'Not yet. The waiting's the hardest part. Don't feel you have to stay.'

'At least let me get you a cup of coffee?'

Just then a man got up to offer his seat to Mal.

'Don't suppose you could sign

something for my wife? She's a big fan of your shows. She went along to your roadshow but couldn't get an auto-graph as it was so busy.'

Mal declined the seat but was happy to sign a page out of his pocketbook and give it to the man. He scrawled his signature in fountain pen.

'If you could write *To Angela?*' the man asked, clearly embarrassed but going there anyway. 'Sorry to disturb you at a tricky time.'

'Not a problem. Happy to help. Is it your wife you're here with?'

'It is. She had a fall at work.'

After Mal had obliged, he repeated the offer of a drink for Amy. She accepted, even though she didn't really want one. She'd rather he just go. Her mind was a mess. She hoped that if she took it, he'd feel he'd done something useful and leave; then she could deal with the situation in peace.

When he returned, however, the seat next to her had been vacated and he sat down.

'Thanks for coming, but honestly I'm fine,' she protested, her fingers being burned as she tried to take the hot plastic cup. She almost dropped it and his hand shot out to steady hers.

'Nearly,' he said.

Her gaze flicked to his, then away as Mal offered a napkin to wrap around the cup. 'An old chef's trick,' he confided. She noticed he had one wrapped around his own.

'You know all the answers, Mal.'

'No. If I did I'd know what to say now, and I don't. Other than that Josie's a good sort, I hear. She's tough and resilient.'

Amy answered softly, 'She used to be homeless, if that's what you mean. Some would say deserving and vulnerable. We should have taken more care of her.'

'Actually, I really don't know all the answers, Amy. Most of it's bluster. Can't you tell?' The comment took her off-guard and she found herself staring at him. 'But I do know you are being way too hard on yourself.'

'So what makes you think you're qualified to butt in?'

'Because maybe being an outsider makes me objective, Amy.' Mal raised an eyebrow.

'I just mean, you're clearly successful and know what to say to get on. But maybe you don't always have the relevant experience — '

Mal smiled. 'Touché. Try not to worry. It won't make this awful situation any better — in fact, it may just make it worse.'

'I just can't stand the idea of Josie getting hurt on our watch.' Her voice wobbled.

'Things happen.' Mal shrugged.

'How can you be so blase about it?'

'Remind me sometime to tell you about when we were filming out in a jungle lightning storm and the cameras nearly went on fire. Or the time my cameraman fell down a crevasse.'

Amy stared. Maybe that was what

celebrity did? Made you take everything for granted — gave you an inflated idea of your own worth. She didn't for a minute believe that just because he'd seen it all and done it all, in the TV sense, that he had a licence to dish out opinions.

'I didn't realise filming cooking shows was so hard core,' she said.

'You'd better believe it. Life can be unpredictable. You can't prepare for every eventuality. So be kind, don't beat yourself up about this. Josie wouldn't want you to.'

'You really think you know what Josie will want?' Amy couldn't dislodge the hard knot of frustration that burned in her chest. 'And I *am* worried. I'm guessing that Lorna told you about her fears — that she suspects it was a faulty piece of equipment in the kitchen.'

'You don't even know that yet, Amy. You can't make snap judgments.'

And yet this was her business. This could be a major hitch. If their property and the workplace had harmed a member of staff, they could have a huge claim lodged against them.

Amy tried to speak more calmly as she went on. 'Call me a pessimist, but it pays to be prepared. We may be responsible. And we'd have to shoulder that, Mal.'

'You really don't know what happened yet. So let's just wait and put everything into wishing Josie a speedy recovery. She's in the best hands.'

Just then a nurse came into the waiting room calling her name.

Mal took the coffee cup from her fingers and Amy jumped to her feet. In moments she was hurrying through the hospital willing Josie to be sitting up in bed and praying that she wasn't being overly optimistic in that hope.

* ★ ★

Amy almost wept with relief when she did find her friend, not sitting up, but lying awake and with colour back in her cheeks. Josie blinked at her and smiled

86

and Amy tried to keep the tears in.

'Are you OK, Jose?' she asked softly.

'I'm fine. Did I give you all a fright?'

'We've all been shedding enough tears to water the herb garden for a week. We were right to worry — you didn't look in a good way.'

The memory alone made her shudder. Especially when paramedics had covered her with a mask and various wires.

'I feel OK. I fainted, apparently. Electric shock. I've been told off by the nurses. I'm really sorry for causing all the trouble.'

Amy felt dread hit the bottom of her stomach like a leaden ball.

'It was my fault,' Josie was saying. 'I just hope it hasn't wrecked Lorna's sockets in the kitchen. She's always telling me not to plug my mobile charger in in the kitchen. I'd run out of charge and left my power bank at home. I thought a ten minutes charge wouldn't hurt. The plug blew me back before I realised what was happening! I don't remember after that.'

Amy could barely believe what she was being told. 'We thought it was the pressure cooker!'

'I hadn't even touched that! It probably isn't a good idea to have my mobile out where there's water and electrics. Lorna's always been strict.'

Amy felt her chest ease slightly. Josie was OK and that was what mattered above all else. Maybe the scare would help her take more care.

'I'm just glad you aren't hurt badly. Lorna can send you to the firing squad for rebel mobile use another time. We're too happy to see you awake and breathing!'

Josie confided, 'That phone of mine has been faulty. I returned it and it was supposed to have been fixed. I won't trust it again now. An excuse to get a new one.'

'Well, you've proved how much we care about you. Everybody's devastated! I think Lorna's shut the café today. She can't work when she's worrying about you.'

'Now that's my fault too!' Tears welled up in Josie's eyes. It was probably relief, mixed with the trauma of waking up in hospital and her earlier shock just hitting home. And the fact she'd had such hard teenage years living on the street probably made them all so much more determined to treat Josie like one of the family.

'You're so lovely. You're like family to me! I'm so lucky to have met you guys.'

Amy leaned in and hugged her friend. 'You're family to us. And we're the lucky ones. Thank goodness, you're OK, Jose. Will you need time in hospital for observation?'

'They think I'll get out later today.'

'I'll be waiting,' said Amy. 'Mal's here too.'

'Mal? He came to wait for me? The famous celebrity chef is outside waiting for me? We haven't even met properly.' Josie gaped at her, clearly more bothered about Mal Donaldson being there than she was about her brush with death.

'Josie. You're a key team member — of course he's here.'

Josie smiled widely. 'Now that's almost worth being thrown across the room by an electric shock fireworks display for!'

'Hardly,' Amy answered. 'And if you try it again, I may reconsider having you as my friend. That's an official warning!' But Amy disproved her words when she followed it up with the warmest hug she'd ever given her dear friend.

* * *

Mal watched Amy end the call to her sister telling Lorna all was well with Josie. It was as if several tons of worry had lifted from her shoulders. She pushed her wild curly hair aside and it bounced back to where it had been. He itched to reach out and do it for her, but he'd never dare.

'Better?'

'A bit.'

She let out a long sigh and he

wondered if he should invite her for a drink. He figured she needed a brandy. He knew she'd never accept.

He couldn't blame her for feeling such responsibility for her business. But at the same time it was apparent this woman shouldered way too much business stress. He knew the feeling too and could relate — running a restaurant brought round-the-clock responsibility. But it really wasn't good for Amy to feel the high-stakes emotional involvement he sensed she had with her business. It was almost as if the negatives outweighed all the positives he so clearly saw.

She was weighing herself down with woes.

'If you don't mind me saying, you do need to chill,' Mal told her. 'Is this a bad time to mention that? Before you get defensive and bite my head off, I mean that as a compliment. Your work ethic is off the scale — but you should do yourself more favours.'

'On what planet is that a compliment exactly?'

'Planet Honest Mal the Straight Talker. The thing is, I sense your uptight disposition. It's coming off you in waves.'

'Well, I have just had an employee in a near-death situation. And I did believe it was our establishment that was at fault.'

'And you were proven wrong. You jumped to the worst case scenario. And it was unfounded.'

'Is this Have-a-go-at-Amy day?'

Mal shook his head and ventured to give her a smile of encouragement. 'Far from it. It's utterly commendable that you take your business so seriously. But where's the joy, Amy? You're losing sight of it completely.'

She didn't answer. He thought he knew why.

'It's your art, isn't it? You can't devote enough of yourself to it and you resent the other stuff that gets in the way. I'm the same with cooking, if that helps.'

Amy nodded curtly but didn't say anything beyond a shrug.

'You love your art. You want to bury yourself up to the neck in it. The other stuff isn't what you love. Am I right?'

'Maybe. It isn't rocket science to work out that art is what fires me. I'm an artist. The clue's in the title. It would be like making you take up waiting instead of cooking the food.' Amy threw him a scathing look. 'What gives you the right to start levelling lots of accusations at me anyway? Or is it just because I'm stuck here you've decided to badger me. Harassment as an added extra to a hospital visit. Nice move, Mal.'

'I just sense that you really don't like the business end of the café. And I'd put money on being right, though I'm really not a betting man. I am right, aren't I?'

'Is it that obvious?' She looked incensed at her own confession.

Mal worried that he'd gone too far. Had he reached too swiftly for the jugular? Might he be harming his future relations with Amy Chambers beyond repair? But the fire in her eyes was dying down a little.

'I never started out on this to end up dealing with a desk job more than anything else,' she said gruffly.

'Business does bring a heavy paperwork burden. But there are ways around it,' Mal persisted.

'And I hate IT. I know how to do it as I learned a bit of graphic design, but I hate administration.'

'I think I got that, Amy.'

He realised he'd lifted the lid on her feelings. A cloud of smoke had poured out that was now surrounding both of them. Amy was suddenly free to let rip on what she really felt.

'It stresses me out. I hate the paperwork. The spreadsheets. Even the website. I hate dealing with customer services and all the rest of it. But I do it all because I'm the one with those skills. Lorna is the chef and Harry is the horticulture-head. So Amy has to pick up the rest. I'm the only one with admin know-how.'

'But all work and no play makes Amy a rather fed-up woman!'

'That makes me sound selfish, Mal.'

'Is it selfish to want as much freedom as the others have and to put yourself first?'

Amy looked at him. Mal fixed his gaze on hers.

'Did you even realise you've been putting up with all this stress and inwardly sulking for years? I've heard the stories from Lorna about Phoebe. That she climbed up a tree for half a day because you wouldn't let her have chocolate. Are you sulking up a tree because you have all these business chores and it's making you unhappy, but you can't risk letting your partners down?

'You don't have to always pick up the pieces and be perfect, Amy. It is allowed to say, no!'

Amy took in her biggest breath yet.

'You mentors — you come in here, throwing your weight around . . . being . . . being right! And don't talk about

Phoebe that way — she can't help the way she is. What's so wrong about going up a tree when it feels right?'

Mal smiled from ear to ear.

'I am right, and at least you're almost admitting it. And that is the biggest step you've taken in a while. We've come on far today.'

He knew she was annoyed and put out by his probing but it was a humoured version of irritation. She might play the tough girl, but underneath she'd known he had a point.

'Can't a girl get on with having a quiet, disgusting hospital coffee in peace without hounding from opinionated celebrity chefs?'

Mal laughed. 'We've barely even started. So — just putting it out there — maybe you need to think about resolving your business issue. Maybe get a part-time administrator on board? One of your homelessness project newbies? Or a college business course graduate? Think that might be an idea, Amy?'

'Point taken, but I'll have to think about it. Maybe I'm not out of my tree yet?'

'OK. First mentoring lesson over. And when you're ready . . . '

Amy pulled a wry face. 'I didn't realise this was a mentoring lesson, Mal.'

'Didn't I tell you? I like to spring things on people when they least expect it, Amy. It's what an effective mentor does — drops a pebble in the pool and then lets things settle by themselves.'

'Unfortunately, it's been a day of those nasty surprises. More rocks than pebbles. I wasn't ready. And I prefer my pools to be ripple-free. Calm waters are my preferred choice.'

'Business always brings ripples, Amy. And my surprises won't be nasty. Hopefully you may even grow to like me. Your business, hopefully, will too,' Mal told her. 'Now come on. Let's go and find a sandwich. My stomach thinks my throat's been cut and my brain can't work without food.'

'You should have that as your catchphrase.'

'Maybe it is already.'

She followed, her shoulders hunched, but he noticed the furrow between her brows wasn't as marked as it had been when he'd got there today — nor when they'd first met. And of that, he was rightly proud and glad.

5

'Can I come over to yours?' Lorna had asked on the phone, surprising Amy.

They'd had a stressful, emotional day with unexpected events, and she'd assumed her sister would rather have an early night with her husband than a get-together. Considering Lorna lived in a quaint, comfy cottage while Amy's place was a tiny, cramped apartment in the eaves above her studio, she also wondered why she hadn't invited her round there.

'When did you ever have to ask?' Amy countered. 'Usually you breeze in to raid my biscuit tin and take command of the remote control. What's different tonight?'

The pause down the line told Amy there was something.

'When I want you to help me.'

'Sounds mysterious. Will there be a

99

glass of wine too?'

'A delicious red Harry bought from Provence. Only the best for my sister. You deserve it after the hospital today.'

'You're on! Come as quick as you can.'

Harry's parents ran an organic lavender farm in France. Every time Amy thought about it she conjured up images of long, hot summers painting. Shades of Van Gogh, quaint French villages and rustic food — perhaps she would become a mad hermit artist let loose in her dreamscape. She loved her life, but she liked the dream too.

* * *

Lorna arrived twenty minutes later brandishing an assortment of bags.

'We're going to make slow cooker marmalade. To sell in the shop. And I wanted time with you, in case you thought I was iffy with you earlier this week.'

'Me, marmalade? The woman who

burns toast?' Amy countered. 'You know we don't have a problem. We're allowed to have tussles from time to time.'

'A slow cooker is a glorified light bulb with cooking dividends, Amy. Even you can manage one. I'll set it all up, then you baby-sit it and check it doesn't burn.'

'Will it need night feeds too?'

Lorna laughed. 'You'll get beauty sleep, don't worry.'

Before her eyes Lorna decanted three slow cookers, a ton of prepped lemons, oranges and limes, plus enough sugar to rot a set of plastic joke teeth.

'Is Paddington Bear coming?'

Lorna laughed. 'It'll use up the fruit glut Harry over-ordered. And everybody loves marmalade. Don't you remember Dad loved it? And Mum used to make it.'

Lorna had been Phoebe's age when their mother passed away. Amy had been younger still.

'I don't remember. But I was only

seven when she died.'

Amy hoped her throat didn't clog. Even talking about it brought up sharp memories that their father had only been gone five years. He had loved his wife to distraction.

'Marmalade memory lane,' declared Lorna. 'I've wanted to do this. Teach you the skills so that one day you'll make marmalade with your kids like Mum did. She'd have wanted it.'

'I don't know what to say. Apart from the fact I may just be an old maid and wreck the plan.'

'You've plenty of life to live. It needn't be awkward to talk about them. We miss them — but we need to remember. It keeps the love alive.'

'You could have warned me. I'd have bought in extra tissues. And my waterproof clothes.'

Lorna smiled though her eyes were misty.

'No tears, just love. But first . . . ' Lorna rolled up her sleeves and grabbed the bottle of red. 'Fetch a glass.' She glugged the wine in the glass then filled another with water.

'Has hell frozen over? You aren't drinking?'

'Driving. Couldn't carry all this stuff here.' Lorna held up a glass. 'To them. Mum and Dad would have wanted us to move forward. They'd have encouraged our hopes for more. And now feels like a good moment to tell you. Harry and I have some news.'

'You don't half go about telling me things the long way.'

Lorna grinned widely with burgeoning pride.

'We're not just expanding the restaurant — we've a baby on the way!'

'That's fabulous. I'm so pleased for you.' Amy had known her sister had wanted to start a family for some time. This news was perfect.

'Hopefully we'll be up and running with the expansion by then. We can get an extra chef in situ. Sound like a plan?'

'No one will match you, of course. Though they may be easier to work with.' Amy winked. 'Calmer. Less prone to theatrics.'

'I have a hope they might be even better. We're all moving forward in all ways.'

'Any preference for a boy or girl?'

'Happy to have a healthy bundle to hug. Harry hasn't stopped smiling.'

Amy hugged her sister close. So pleased for her, so genuinely happy. And just wishing in a tiny corner of her heart that she really was moving forward. Instead of feeling at sea, with a life she loved but which was, if she truly admitted it, sometimes lonely.

Theirs was a business that took almost all their energy and left scant time for social life. Mal was right about the admin, she had resented it for a while. And forget romantic notions. She could count the number of times she'd worn a dress in the last two years — let alone had her hair styled. Maybe she needed to reconsider and reclaim some space?

She sipped her wine and made a

promise to try harder.

'This momentous, commemorative marmalade will be an exceptional vintage,' Lorna proclaimed.

'A classic to treasure.'

If only her life was as promise-filled too.

★ ★ ★

'How's the new place?' Lorna asked. 'How are you finding Derbyshire after all the time you've spent globe-trotting and city-dwelling? How do we measure up?'

Mal looked up from the grill pan he was using to create something that smelled mouth-wateringly Oriental.

'I'm loving it. But the hotel's only temporary. I'm also looking at rented property now.'

'Why not just stay where you are?'

'A short lease would suit. I have business interests to sort out locally.'

Lorna didn't say more, so he felt the need to explain. 'I inherited a business premises from my uncle. But it's in a state of disrepair; I'd originally intended selling it because of work commitments. Now I'm considering restoring and refurbishing it myself. It's a surprise undertaking even for me.'

Lorna nodded. 'Sounds impressive. If you need help finding a short let just shout. Get Amy's friend Beth on the job. She's an eagle-eyed estate agent. They deal with lettings too.'

Amy had just walked in and he watched as she eyed them both suspiciously, as if she thought they'd been sharing scurrilous tales about her.

'Mal needs Beth. Urgently.'

Amy nodded. 'My friend Beth will just love to hear that. Especially as she's already told me she thinks you're hot property — and not in the bricks and mortar sense. Unfortunately her burly fireman boyfriend might not approve of you making any offers, even if she does.'

Mal laughed. 'You can be funny when you try. Ever thought about stand-up?'

Amy pulled a wry expression.

'Thanks. I spend all night writing lines to impress you. Is that all the thanks I get?'

Why, Mal wondered, did Amy Chambers always deflect people? And would he ever find out more? Why she was so shy? So hard to get a straight gaze from?

Lorna continued, 'Mal's on the lookout to move from the Old Mill to a let.'

'Want me to get Beth round?'

He saw that her cheeks were coloured.

'If she wouldn't mind, it might help.'

'She'll be here breaking speed limits during her lunch hour. Should I warn the police?'

'Tell her to drive slowly or I won't make her lunch. But yes, it'd certainly help to have somebody scout for me. Back to business. Can we have a catch-up?'

They went through to the back office and discussed current priorities. Mal pushed a stack of papers in front of them. 'My report.'

Lorna stared at the wedge of paper in awe.

'You've been busy.'

'Now, if anything doesn't fit we refine things. This is not about ego or me taking the lead. It's pointers for progress.

'Hopefully by the end of the month we could have contractors finishing off the extension. The main issue I have is suggesting we do the lease rooms differently so that they can be flexible rather than fixed — more options, I figured. Have a look then tell me what you think.

'I also think the art workshop space needs to be bigger because I'm thinking long term. Bigger classes down the line. My first aim is to get started on the education centre planning. The short let rooms are secondary.'

'There's an added thing on the to-do list,' said Lorna. 'I'll need a replacement chef.'

'This is news,' said Mal. 'Nothing wrong?'

'Far from it.' Lorna's smile was wide. 'An extra crew member, permanent and full-time. Only this one won't do much except drink milk and look cute for a while.' She nodded to her tummy.

The penny dropped for Mal and he couldn't stop smiling. Especially as he saw the happy, loving look her younger sister sent her.

'Congratulations, Lorna. A business baby and a real one. You're really pushing forward. In all ways.'

'Cheek! Don't talk about pushing. You'll put me off. But we will need an extra chef.'

So far Mal had outlined ideas which had largely only built on finessing and tweaking. He'd encouraged segmenting their market to consider business lunches and group bookings. And his big suggestion was a separate room with multimedia technology focusing on special events but flexible enough to accommodate meetings, weddings and groups. They might even consider private dining that would double up as a gallery space. Hence the need to revisit the layouts. It could even offer small conference potential.

A more formalised partnership with a local college was Mal's key wish. He hoped they'd concur.

Amy explained, 'I already have a contact at the school. Though I know people at the college. I'm in touch with the Additional Support Unit who come in for art therapy.'

'Maybe we could get together to work out a strategy on formalising? Shall we work together on that?' He tried to hook Amy's gaze but she evaded him. 'How's Phoebe?' he asked.

Her gaze latched in pronto.

'Her mum tells me she's having a hard time at school. I try to help, as her mum has a lot on her plate. I agreed to go in to school with her.'

'If there's anything I can do?' He closed in. He saw her awkward reaction to his move but he couldn't help himself. She had the power and magnetism to make him want to know more. To help somehow.

Amy shook her head. 'No — but thank you.'

'If Phoebe ever wants to hang out — send her to see me in the kitchen and I'll get her cooking.'

'Unfortunately I can't do that. You'd need full disclosure and background checks for the befriending agency I work for. Child protection stuff.'

'Ah. Of course. Sorry. That's a pretty amazing thing to do.'

'Don't be sorry. That would be lovely, and if you don't mind having me there too I'll suggest it in the future. Sometimes you just want to do some good for those who need it. Thank you for the offer. You may need ear plugs when she starts to talk non-stop.'

Her gaze lifted to meet his and he was glad that she held it. Progress. Slow but significant.

'I can handle it,' he said. 'I have a sister who's the same. In fact I think she could probably take Phoebe on and win.'

Amy answered, 'There's something I

should mention about Phoebe . . . '

Her heart beat fast but there was no getting away from the need to say this.

Mal searched her tortured face, then put his hand on hers. 'You don't need to explain. It's fine. Phoebe is fine without me knowing details. Accepted without background knowledge.'

Amy was taken aback. 'She has Asperger's Syndrome and ADHD. She's high functioning on the autistic spectrum. Sometimes she can't cope with her situations.'

'I had a cousin with similar issues. He was a big part of my life so you don't need to put her in a box for my benefit. No need for warnings.'

Amy stared at Mal as if he'd just offered her moon dust truffles. She clearly hadn't expected his response.

'Look, I'd really like to chat and understand the art side of the business better. You could invite me to watch you at your potter's wheel or making something public-arty?'

'Public-arty? Is that a real word?'

He nudged her with his elbow.

'See, I need your technical expertise to help with jargon.'

She sighed. 'Drop in. Though don't blame me if you get splashed.'

'I may bring you baked goods as inducement.'

'That really wouldn't work.' She nailed him with eyes so blue and deep he felt enchanted. 'Carbs make me angry. Like Gremlins with water. One doughnut and it gets ugly. You wouldn't want to see that. And I couldn't be held responsible.'

He grinned. 'I just might.'

'Don't bring carbs. If you want to see me work, you have to play by rules.'

Mal saluted. 'Amy in command. That's more exciting than you realise.'

The fact she was blushing tickled him no end.

★ ★ ★

The radio blared some fast-paced song but Amy didn't hear a word or a note. She was still trying to figure out Mal's earlier confession that he understood additional needs. He was more of a surprise and an enigma combined than ever.

She tried to disguise how her hands shook and her insides twirled. She'd never let Mal Donaldson know how powerfully he affected her.

Mr Super Cool Chef with his dancing eyes and Yorkshire accent had surprised her with his offers to help. What she didn't know was why he'd done it, or indeed how she felt. Why would he care? Or try to befriend either her or Phoebe? Was he being over-nice to get around her sharp edges?

Whatever the motive Phoebe was a complicated child whose issues he'd no idea about. To the uninitiated she was just a talkative, eager kid who liked to speak her mind. Her ADHD meant she yearned to be on the go and found concentrating tricky, often leaping from one activity to the next without enjoying anything at all.

Her learning style was over-thinking.

She'd get so enthusiastic about something she loved that she'd go OTT and straight into meltdown at the slightest setback. Her Asperger's Syndrome brought complex behaviours that needed a deft touch.

Mal appeared with two coffee mugs and a roguish grin. 'No cakes or biscuits. Didn't want to get another warning. Or worse.'

She breathed in deeply, grateful for the perk up. 'Coffee smells good.'

'Only the best.' He grinned. That expression, a mix of dashing gentleman and naughty little boy, made her stomach flip. She told herself it was only because he was a hot man and she wasn't used to those. She needed to get a grip.

He sat down on the stool by her desk. 'Great vase, I love the shape. You make those?'

'For the art shop. Our bestseller.'

The shape was an organic, wavy design with a wider base. It was a higher price point. When she'd opened up the pottery store she'd expected to have to pay the rent with touristy items. Yet years later, here she was selling pieces she loved like a real artist. This was so much better than being a city college art tutor.

'The design is called Phoebe. Like her, each is totally individual and speaks up for itself.'

'I think my sister would love one. Could I place an order?'

'Any colour you like.'

'Yellow. She loves a splash of something bright. She's called Daisy.'

'You do strike me as a splash of colour person.'

'I tend to wear blue or grey.'

'You have red sports shoes. Your car is red. Your phone, too.'

'You noticed that?'

'My training is in the detail. You had a red jacket on when we met at the pond. We all hint at what we like subconsciously.' She felt she'd admitted too much and Mal, sensing her discomfort, changed the subject.

'It's a great village. Enid in the shop gets all overexcited when I buy a paper.

She's taken to keeping me chocolate bars. I like it here.'

'Yes, I remember you said you want to rent here. The community council will go wild. A celebrity in situ for the summer fete. Christmas has come early!'

'I've some work underway at Darwin Fields. My London restaurant and flat are on the market now. Last year I spent time in France and I'd planned moving there for a change. After so much time filming abroad I needed time out. I've realised coming back here would help me regroup. I'm planning to refurbish my uncle's old place.'

'You should speak to Harry. His parents live in Provence.'

'Funnily enough I stayed in St Remy. Hiding away from a relationship that had gone sour.'

Amy took his confession in.

'I know that feeling.'

'You too?'

'It brought me here.' Amy shrugged. 'Had a man in my life. Unfortunately he moved on when it suited him. Left me feeling I couldn't work out which way was up. Then a chance came up to come here, so I didn't think twice.'

Mal held her gaze. Then he held up his coffee mug. 'Here's to moving on and expanding both our horizons. We're better than that.'

Amy nodded. 'Do you think there's a gap in the market for an arts hub/ bistro type thing here?'

'Of course. Or I wouldn't be here. Tonight Lorna and I will join forces to experiment with prepping dishes for the improved menu. I'd welcome your views. I'll even keep the carb count low.'

She smiled. 'I'm not that great a dinner guest but I could be tempted. What I mentioned earlier about Phoebe — I have the same problems to some degree. I had ADHD. I thought I was just a failure at school until my dad pushed to get it diagnosed. I've also always found the social thing taxing. I think there's some Asperger's in me too. So working with Phoebe is really important — not just because I know her mum needs me. Not everybody is accepting, unfortunately.'

'I don't care what people think. That's their problem. To be honest I find the in-your-face 'here's what I think' approach refreshing. Especially after my prior career life. OK?'

Amy nodded, hoping he wasn't one of those people who said it would be OK then looked appalled later. She'd met a few of those.

'People with Asperger's syndrome see, hear and feel the world differently. Though they're now re-evaluating the terminology of that too.'

'I think you're both incredible people. Maybe put down that stick you beat yourself up with? I utterly respect what you're doing to help her and now I understand why.'

She wiped her stained hands on her overalls and looked into the middle distance.

'I must get on. I've had another vase order now. Busy, busy.' She nodded towards the pad she'd just written down his vase requirements on. 'You'd best get back into the kitchen or Lorna will track you down.'

'I won't risk that. A pregnant woman on the war path is not something I want to think about.'

Amy watched her studio door close behind him. Mal was even more surprising than she could have imagined.

In a good way. In a very good way indeed.

6

In just over a week Mal had trans-
formed their café kitchen from a rustic
but serviceable space to a high-tech
bistro-ready catering-creation space.

Equipment had been moved; Amy
wondered how Lorna would deal with
this development. Yet when she looked
to her sister she was mid-laugh and
enthusing over some dish she'd tasted.

Mal was achieving miracles already.
Despite her reservations Amy had to
admit the layout looked better. She'd
called Phoebe's mum and explained
that Mal had suggested inviting Phoebe
for a tasting party if she was free. Her
charge had arrived twenty minutes
later.

Menu items crammed the work-
bench. They'd been given small score
cards and tasting spoons to rate each
dish. Was this how they did things in

top-class eateries?

Phoebe made it her mission to sample each dish. She enthused, 'The pasta is delicious! And the veggie burger is super good.'

'Good! I designed that one for Amy.' Mal winked her way.

Phoebe's eyes widened. 'Does that mean she gets them free for lunch whenever she wants?'

'We have to keep some for the customers,' pointed out Lorna.

Amy saw that Phoebe watched Mal as if he performed magic tricks; she was clearly besotted. Was that how she'd acted when Jason had burst into her life full of energy, spirit and promise?

She ducked from the sharp memories. Knowing now it had all been fake.

But she'd seen that look before when Joanna, her ex's next in line, had fallen for Jason. OK, this time it was ten-year-old hero-worship over adult infatuation, but it still threw Amy's emotions back to brutal heartbreak. It brought back memories of the signs that had stared at her starkly. She'd been a stepping-stone to the biggest prize. Joanna Davenport, the college's latest asset, had been his goal all along.

And suddenly the way Phoebe acted, as if Mal was the best thing since sliced bread toasted and sugar sprinkled, rankled. Which was ridiculous. He wasn't Jason. Phoebe wasn't Joanna. She just felt like an onlooker again.

'This spaghetti is amazing, Mal. I'll have to get the recipe for my mum.' There was sauce smeared on the child's chin. Phoebe's appetite for life, attention and food were fierce.

Mal's eyes twinkled. 'What does Amy think?'

'It is good. Though a little rich for my tastes.'

He turned on the spot and pointed a spatula at her. 'Is that the best you can do? Good?'

Amy found the pasta was hard to swallow. And it was perfectly cooked. It was she who was overwrought by the man's intense attention. She took a cleansing sip of her water.

'Can I have more?' Phoebe asked.

Mal grinned. 'Course. There's plenty.'

Amy cautioned, 'Just not so much that you're sick. Or you'll spoil your dessert. Not so much Parmesan cheese this time.'

Although the café was largely vegan, they were also offering non-vegan options.

Mal grinned. 'And dessert involves meringues so you wouldn't want to miss out.'

Amy saw Mal wink at her again. She wished he wouldn't. She could never do kitchen flirting again. She'd trusted her mentor once before, and her only reward was burned fingers and the realisation that three was a crowd.

As Phoebe replenished her bowl, Amy had had her fill — of memories, and of feeling like a fool.

'I'll just do some bookkeeping work in the corner,' she said and turned her focus elsewhere.

★   ★   ★

Phoebe's mum collected her with much praise of Mal and his attentions. The kitchen staff had taken over the clearing up when Mal took two coffees and sat down on the bench opposite Amy.

'Did the menu pass muster?'

'Of course. A definite hit. I'd expect no less.'

'Thanks for getting Phoebe here.' His eyes danced as he watched her.

'I knew she'd enjoy it.'

'And thanks for getting Beth on the case. She's already lined up properties for me to look at. She's something. She's also taking a look at my uncle's place; she has local architect and contractor contacts. So you really helped me out.'

'Beth's a great friend. And now she won't have to go on at me about how wonderful you are. She's had you all to herself.'

'Well, that would be tricky. Because I'm well aware you don't find me wonderful. Do you, Amy? This issue that rumbles between us has to get dealt with. Why the back-off earlier? I saw you freeze and retreat. I couldn't work out why.'

She pushed her papers together and looked up, ready to defend herself.

'I don't know what you mean.'

'You tensed up earlier when we were talking to Phoebe.'

'I didn't.'

'Trust me, you did. And I know I haven't done anything. Which leads me to think somebody once did something you haven't got over. And you're shutting everybody out because of it. Lorna mentioned someone called Jason . . . '

'Do not even go there! Just because you're helping us doesn't mean you can tread anywhere you choose.' Amy clenched her hands around her coffee cup, considering throwing it at him or the wall. Somehow he'd seen through her coping mechanisms.

'Sorry, but . . . '

Her eyes snapped to his. 'It's not up for discussion. And it's none of your business.' She scrubbed at her temple.

'Trust someone who's been hurt too to guess.'

She clicked her laptop shut and tried to remind herself she could meet his gaze without blushing.

He pulled her laptop out of the way to stop her fiddling with it. Their fingers brushed. Amy felt electricity and attraction she was helpless to ignore. But she'd learned of the dangers of that.

'Don't be so jumpy, Amy. You make me paranoid that I'm so awful you can't stand being near me. What happened, Amy? What did he do?'

Amy felt anger tumble out that she was powerless to control.

'I can't go there. Look, I know you're only trying to break the ice but I really have no desire to do this. Please respect my wishes.'

'You can't keep it all locked away forever. Especially when it keeps making you freeze up. You have to let it go sometime,' Mal said softly.

But Amy turned away, knowing she was on the verge of crying but keeping the tears in and her back straight. Tonight had made her feel weak and foolishly willing. And desperate for any solace she could find . . . which equalled danger.

* ★ ★

Sometimes, Amy reflected next morning, watching her sister and her husband bantering like kids, she did miss male company. Though she'd never had a relationship like her sister's.

'Stop it! Stop flicking me with your tea towel. Or there will be consequences,' Harry warned.

Amy rolled her eyes and commented, 'Can you two please quit — it's giving me a headache.'

'If she doesn't cease and desist she'll be sleeping in the greenhouse. Or by the compost.'

'You wouldn't dare!' Lorna said, then threw bubbles from the sink at his back.

'Try me.'

'Can't either of you pack it in?' Amy said, exasperated, and walked out. She'd no doubt that, left alone, they'd soon be cuddling. And her sister was the worst culprit.

But she loved her Harry to distraction; they'd met at a party in a London pub and had been inseparable ever since. Harry had dreams of working as a garden designer but since coming into business together he'd gone fully into organic produce, importing and running the veg shop. Which he did with brilliant efficiency.

Amy walked around the herb garden picking rosemary and lavender. She sniffed, closed her eyes and breathed deeply.

'Hey,' said a voice nearby. 'Lorna said you'd staged a protest and vacated the area.'

Butterflies spun in her tummy at the male voice and Amy turned defensively.

But it was Dean Harper, who worked as a courier driver and collected her special delivery items. He'd become an acquaintance, if not quite a friend, and Amy recognised the signs that he might just like her. Like the fact he sometimes just stood and didn't talk.

'They're acting like little kids.' Amy shrugged towards the kitchen.

'You need to escape this place more. Come out with me — new place in the High Street. Oriental Buffet — fancy it?'

'You know I'm vegan.'

He nodded. 'Already checked with them. They offer at least five dishes that are dairy and egg free, and veggie.'

'Five. You have been thorough.'

Dean smiled at the compliment. Enthusiasm shone from him like a light in a glass jar. 'So — I have a voucher and it doesn't have to be a date or anything.'

'Platonic, pure and simple?'

'You deserve to have a nice time, Amy.'

'OK, Dean — you're on.' Half of her brain thought *What am I messing with?* The other part had lately recognised she did need to get out again. Mal had shown her she wasn't yet over Jason. Maybe she needed to be bolder?

Dean punched the air and Amy swiftly regretted her decision. She gave him a stern stare.

'I get it. Just let me be happy you agreed. I don't expect anything. But we get on well, Amy, and you deserve someone to look out for you.'

'Sorry to interrupt,' said a voice nearby. Mal wore an ultra-serious face for once. Had he overheard their entire conversation?

Dean didn't look too pleased. He didn't step back or take his hand from Amy's elbow.

Amy prompted, 'I need to talk to Mal, Dean. I'll see you later.'

'I can wait,' Dean offered.

'I have firing to see to next. I'll text you.'

'Don't go inventing reasons not to let me take you out.' Dean nodded to Mal, who let him pass, and then glanced her way. 'A yes is non-negotiable.'

Mal's jaw twitched as he waited.

'I have the new menu leaflets from the printers. Thought you'd want to see the new corporate logo and style in your hand.'

'Oh. Thank you. Sure, I'll take a look.'

She knew she sounded dismissive. But she hated the way she'd just felt, as if she'd been found out. And it bothered her that Mal watched her in such a stern manner, as if she owed him some explanation. And none of what she was feeling made any sense at all . . . unless she admitted that Mal mattered or cared.

'How about coffee in your workshop? I also have admin to run by you. And yes, he likes you. It's very obvious, from where I'm watching. So if you want my view, you should leave well alone.'

Amy gaped. 'That's none of your business.'

Mal breathed deeply. 'If you don't want to date him, tell him. Or you'll give the wrong signals.'

'What I want is not to be preached to by people who've no right. Get off your high horse and stick your nose into somebody else's business.'

And with that she turned and stalked

away in the ultimate stroppy-kid tantrum. Clearly Phoebe was rubbing off
on her.

And only a few seconds later, Amy
couldn't quite believe she'd messed up
so badly with her mentor so soon.

7

'Knock, knock. Amy. Have you calmed down yet?'

Mal's tone bothered her. Even when in the wrong, his voice registered an attraction hit. Amy had never before realised her weakness for Yorkshiremen. Or her serial weakness for men in the restaurant trade.

'Maybe. But listen . . . '

'Don't say it. I know — I shouldn't have stuck my nose in; I'd no right. You were completely justified to tell me to buzz off.'

She turned to stare him down. She probably still looked riled — he'd overstepped — but she too regretted her overreaction.

'Remind me never to get your back up again. You're scary when your blood's up.'

'So don't cross me and we'll do fine.'

She smiled thinly.

Mal raised his chin and nodded. 'The trouble is . . . I do think you could do better than Dean Harper. Even if it's not my place.'

'You don't know him.' She pushed at her curls.

'Actually, I do. He's a regular in the Dog and Ferret. I've taken to going there to read the paper and use the wi-fi at night. He boasts with his mates about his skills with women. So it bothers me when a future prospect is you.'

Amy sucked in air. 'He's just a guy who's asked me out and worn me down. He's not my type anyway.'

Mal was close. She smelled his fresh scent.

'So, say no. Just a suggestion; not a command. And why say yes today, anyway?'

Amy wished he wouldn't put her through this. She hated digging into her emotions. She also hated the fact that when Mal talked to her, her pulse upped.

'Ever consider it might be nice for me

to actually wear something that isn't paint or clay-spattered and do my hair like a grown-up instead of being Amy the mad potter? Maybe I just fancied going out in public socially with a man for the first time in eons? Is that what you wanted me to admit?' She was breathing hard. Her chest rose and fell. Venting wasn't just awkward, it was irksome.

His gaze nailed hers. 'I'd have happily obliged. And hopefully given you a better time.'

'I really don't think that's wise, as project partners, do you?'

'Amy, I'm new here. I'd quite like to prove I can still be good company even after spending nearly a year hiding out in St Remy. At least you can trust me.'

She shrugged. 'I've said yes to Dean.'

Mal stared at her so hard she thought her heart might squeak in her chest. 'You're out of his league. I honestly beg you to cancel.'

Just then a furry cannonball burst into Amy's studio with muddy paws that told of time spent up to no good in the veg patch with Harry.

'Watch out, Elgar's mucky!' Amy called — too late. Moments later Mal's beige trousers were covered in modern dog art.

'Sorry.'

'Hey boy, where've you been hiding? Carrotsville?' He rubbed the dog's neck to a rapturous reaction. 'As recompense, your mistress is going to get her coat.'

Amy looked non-plussed.

'Because you need a walk. And we're going out for a breather. Fresh air. You're going to take me over to that airfield and tell me all your stories. And I'll leave these menus and correspondence here and you can get back to me when you have a view. You coming?' He turned. Walked away. Then threw her a smile over his shoulder. 'Say yes, if you don't want to disappoint your mentor.'

Something inside her conceded that the thought of time with Mal was way more appealing than time with Dean.

She wanted proper adult time. And she also wanted to say yes to his offer.

She grabbed her coat. 'Fine. You win.'

'That wasn't so hard.'

The butterflies answered in unison that they completely agreed. She wanted to get to know Mal Donaldson — the real man and not the hype.

★ ★ ★

They toured the air museum at High Marsh Airfield and before Amy knew it, thirty minutes had turned into nearly two hours. Mal had been very taken with the place and warmly welcomed by its quirky plane enthusiast manager Hugh Tarvey.

Part of Amy regretted losing Mal to Hugh's passion for his pastime. The two men hit it off like kindred spirits. But Hugh was an infectious force in his own right, who loved nothing better than entertaining visitors with his animated script.

When they'd finished their tour he offered them a cup of tea in his hangar.

Amy was tempted to plead the need to finish her work, but she felt she owed Mal the indulgence. Elgar sniffed happily around. She felt like the odd one out.

'You stay, Mal. I'll take Elgar back and you can come back later.'

'It's fine, I'd better let you get back. But I'm in awe of the whole thing. It's like stepping into a fascinating story-book. Quite a place you've got.' His face was bright as they walked away. 'What a guy. He's something, isn't he?'

'He's living his dream. When it comes to planes Hugh has the passion, all right. You never told me your parents were enthusiasts too. I heard you tell him about it.'

Mal nodded. 'They were. They died when I was young. I still have Dad's aircraft books. In fact, this gives me an idea of where to donate them. Do you think Hugh would want them?'

'I'm sorry for your loss, Mal. And I'm sure Hugh would love it. But think it over. I'm sure they still have many memories you may wish to keep.'

'My parents would have loved it here. I think that's why I'm so taken — he reminds me of my dad. So absorbed in it, yet happy to share the world. I sense my dad would have been moving here and offering to be a volunteer guide like Hugh.' She watched him look around in wonder. This was the most animated she'd seen him.

'Well, Hugh says you can come by any time you want.'

'I will. This place will make a great cooking show venue. That's already got me thinking.'

'Don't say anything to Hugh yet. He gets very over-excited. He'll be over the moon at the thought of his precious baby being put on the map, so I'd hate for him to be disappointed.'

'I mean it, Amy. I really think this could work. Of course I'll have a word with my agent but I know our locations manager really well and I'm sure she'd see the merit. Oh my days . . . what is that?'

She already knew. The outline was pretty unmissable. She'd spent long enough crafting it with a soldering iron, and even longer out here putting it painstakingly together, years before.

'That would be my *Sky King*. I told you I do public art. Well, he's one of mine. My tribute to my dad. And to the museum.'

Her *Sky King* graced the hillside like a monarch surveying his lands. A gleaming silver modern structure skeleton, a mesh of steel, was formed into the shape of an old biplane body. It had been her first public art piece after moving here. Generally it had been well received.

Shining in the sunlight, it looked poised to zoom off to horizons new.

'Yours? I never realised you were this brilliant,' Mal stated simply.

'Who else would be crazy enough to build a futuristic biplane on a hill?'

'I love it.'

'That's good. Because so do I. Even Hugh does. And at first he was a tough sell. He wanted a scale model and came armed with historic documents. We found a compromise in the end.'

They walked. Suddenly, somehow they'd fallen into an easy silence. She felt him watch her but didn't dare meet his gaze.

'You can actually stand inside it,' she offered. 'There's a small stair, so you can get in and see what it felt like to fly it. Want to try?'

'When the artist went to so much effort to give me the privilege, would I forgo the chance?'

She hoped his tall frame would fit inside and was glad when he emerged unscathed. But he didn't say anything for longer than she'd like.

'Don't speak, I just want to feel it,' he told her.

Her heart pounded at the words. She felt some strong connection and wanted to observe, to marvel and to just feel it and let it be.

Watching Mal walk around her thirty-foot structure, angled to look as if it was heading off into the sky, she felt she was in the presence of two awesome forces.

And the one that filled her with the most hope and promise was the man beside her.

'You're something.'

'It's my job. Don't go all overcome on me. It's no different to yours.'

'It's very different. Mine is driven by appetite. Yours is a gift, a talent. And an inspiration.'

'In that case, since I'm so brilliant, you can round up Elgar, then take me back for tea and cake,' Amy said. 'Hugh can talk for England but he doesn't have biscuits and now I'm peckish.'

'I think there's some beetroot chocolate cake with your name on it! Your word is my command. C'mon, boy!' They heard the dog bark in the distance and saw him approach at speed.

When he lunged at Mal he told the lively animal, 'Don't want to keep your mistress waiting. She's something when she's on the warpath. Though I'm sure you'll know that already.'

He chuckled as she tried to swat him and they all walked back together.

★ ★ ★

Mal's yellow Phoebe vase was one of her best. And it ended up being a mixture of yellows and purple because somehow the thing had taken on a life of its own and she'd ended up with a piece of magic. She could only hope her mentor and his sister would approve. She'd keep it for her herself if he objected, but she hoped he wouldn't.

'C'mon, Elgar, you need a bath. You smell really bad.'

Elgar looked up at her with milk chocolate eyes and jumped up on the bench where Mal's vase sat . . . knocking it to smash across the floor.

'Elgar!' A gasp caught in her throat as Mal appeared in the doorway.

'Why are you shouting?'

'Your vase is wrecked. I'm so sorry.'

'Don't worry. I'm sorry for you.' He

hunkered down beside her to pick up the pieces.

'I'll get a dustpan,' she said, lest he get hurt on the shards.

When she returned he said softly, 'Lunch tomorrow. Off premises. You and me; I need to get to know you properly because otherwise I can't stop trying to work you out. And that's non-negotiable.'

She gulped, afraid of this leap in their relationship. And his new, intimate, insistent tone.

'OK.' She returned her attention to their task, ultra-aware of their proximity. Of the tantalising smell of him up close . . . lime, lemon? She knew she liked it. Their fingers brushed. And they fumbled as they went for the same pieces of clay. She heard him let out a breath.

Their gazes met and held, and she saw his lips open to say something.

The spell was broken by Lorna's voice.

'Beth's on the line, Mal. She's found

a place that's just come in to let.'

Amy stood up as if electrified and Mal shot up to stand beside her.

'Tell her I'll call her in a couple of minutes on my mobile. We need to bathe this dog first or we'll all die of toxic fume inhalation.'

Elgar went to bolt so Mal grabbed him swiftly. The dog began licking his face. Mal lay back and let Elgar force him to the ground with his lick attack.

Lorna laughed heartily and if she'd sensed their interrupted moment, she didn't allude to it.

Forgetting what had gone before, Amy said, 'This calls for fumigation and a deep cleaning army. And that's just for Mal's clothes.'

★   ★   ★

At half-past twelve next day he stood at the door of her workshop and gave her a pointed stare.

'Ready? Dressed up like a grown-up, I hope?'

146

She grabbed her things. 'Just jeans and a shirt but they're clean and I've even washed my hair. Where are we going?'

Mal slanted his head. 'You're the local girl. But I still aim to try to surprise you.'

'You've got more riddles than the world's biggest joke book, Mal Donaldson.'

He reached out to take a tendril of her hair.

'You should let your go-with-the-flow side out to play more often. I'm guessing we've bonded, now that I'm privy to your inner backchat.'

'We've bonded. Like Elgar's dog hair sticks to my best coat. Somehow it's happened.'

Mal laughed and winked as they walked out of The Hideaway to who knew where.

Actually he did know. But he enjoyed teasing her and filling their time together with suspense. He loved her awkward shyness. That she didn't preen, flirt or know a script with a man. It made her refreshing.

They arrived at Infinity And Beyond Burgers by the side of the road. When he turned to her, she smiled.

'Been here before?'

'I know the guy at the griddle. My old pal, Stan.'

Disappointment slapped Mal down. He'd hoped to take Amy to vegan paradise, to spend solo time with her. Now she'd found an ally.

'How do you know Stan?'

'He runs a watercolour evening class in the village. Hey, Stan — great to see you.'

'And you.' Stan turned back to Mal with a smile. 'Thanks for coming. I've reserved you my best table. Even bought a posy at the florist's.'

Mal whispered, 'He only has three tables. But it pays to be organised so I booked one.'

'So, you're up for the vegan burger challenge then? Both of you?' The poster behind Stan's head declared his large Veganissima burger challenge, with a free meal token to anybody who could complete the feat.

'As if,' said Amy. 'And he's not even vegan.'

'I can do meat-free. And I've been telling Stan about your expansion and the new chef role at The Hideaway. Consider this an informal note of interest.'

'You boys work fast.' Her shock was tangible.

'He has some great ideas, may I add.'

'What about the truck? Would you sell?'

Stan nodded to Mal. 'Yes. But I have options.'

There was a pause while they all digested the revelations and listened to the veg burgers hissing on the hotplate. Stan's skilled hands added bright salad garnish to their plates.

'Have I overstepped again?' Mal checked.

'No. You just move fast.'

'Managed to take you out before

Dean, didn't I? I've learned in business that sometimes you just have an instinct and you should go with it.'

Was he talking about business or her?

Stan grinned as he presented their meals and Amy gaped at the plateful.

Mal picked up the burger bap and took in a preparatory breath. 'I have a feeling we may need roadside assistance to get home after this one — let's give it all we've got.'

She started laughing and couldn't stop. He couldn't have hoped for more.

★　★　★

Amy knew as soon as she got into Dean's car that she'd made a grave error. Not just because since the Veganissima, she'd had no appetite for days. As soon as she smelled aftershave, a voice in her head said, *too much*.

She and Dean were light years apart in many things, but personal scent strength would forever after remain their biggest problem. Maybe it was a warning to get out now?

Dean's car was fast, shiny and leather-seated. Just like him; show over substance.

'You look beautiful,' he told her. As if she'd donned a scarlet velvet gown and jewels. All she'd done was wear flat knee-high boots with a skirt and a round-necked sweater.

'Thanks.'

He'd really gone to some effort and she didn't quite know what to say. He wore a shirt, tie, shiny shoes and cufflinks.

'You look great. Maybe I'm not dressed fancily enough.'

'I asked for a table at the quiet end, away from the high street window.'

Would he rather not be seen out with her?

'I don't like people watching as they pass. Good move,' she said.

'I just wanted an intimate ambience. Privacy.'

The word hung heavy. So did his cologne. She hoped she'd get through the date migraine-free.

The restaurant was very pleasant with

a modern interior and smiling staff. The dimmed lighting lent itself to couple-style dining.

Amy wished she'd got out when she could, or opted for somewhere light, airy and 'less this'. She took the menu, glad for something else to reflect on, other than her own misgivings.

'I know what I'm having. I looked at the menu online,' he told her.

This wasn't a date, yet it felt too much like one. She kept measuring it up against the laughter-filled lunch with Mal, who'd been full of surprises.

She didn't want to date a guy who pre-selected his courses and wore cufflinks for a bite in town.

'Dean, I hate to throw cold water on this — it's a lovely place but I just want to reiterate . . . '

The sight of a familiar figure approaching over the heads of the others in the restaurant through the window left further words stalled on her lips.

Mal was on his way in. With a leggy brunette.

'I know what you're going to say. It's not a date. Message received. Doesn't mean I can't still try to treat you nice. Amy. Please, for once in your life, just go with the moment and let a guy try to woo you.'

Please. Not here. Not now.

'I really don't want to be wooed. I don't even think I'm woo-able.'

Especially now that her mentor was two tables over. He gave her a brief nod to indicate acknowledgement and then his attention returned fully to his date. His jaw flexed. Was he annoyed at her being here? Or narked she was impinging on his date? Had he fixed up an assignation as a protest at her still seeing Dean?

Who was the mystery woman, anyway? Someone he'd met locally? She didn't look local. Maybe a girlfriend from back home? Maybe he had a new love interest. Maybe she'd never know.

'Isn't that your business mogul? What's he like, anyway? I hear he's loaded.'

'Is he? He's pretty down to earth.'

'Don't you read the papers, Amy? He has some posh place in Chelsea. And he's had a fair few high profile ladies on his arm. Lucky guy. Anyway, back to us. What're you ordering?'

'The veg pasta. Sounds yummy. Nice menu.'

'Not as good as your place will be. Go on, have a starter. We want to make the most of this.'

They ordered. And Dean took care and fussed over ordering wine he wouldn't be drinking because he was driving.

'I really don't want any.' A knot tightened in the pit of her stomach.

Dean teased her with a mocking grin. 'I promised you a good night out. Enjoy it. Please.'

'I really don't want to drink.' Inside, frustration whirled as she longed for an opportunity to escape. She didn't want a starter. Or a drink, or to prolong this further. She didn't want to see Mal schmooze a woman when he'd not so long ago taken her out.

She'd so much rather have been at home with a novel, Elgar and a cosy blanket. Even Scrabble by the fireside was way better than this.

Her eyes lifted to mesh with Mal's as he looked up. She tried to let her gaze slide away but it betrayed her by drifting back and he was still watching.

Her pulse hammered. She felt sweat bead on her back. Which was crazy. Her sweater was light and cool and she wasn't prone to hot moments.

'You're miles away . . . I was telling you about my next choice of car,' said Dean.

'Sorry . . . please. Do start again.'

Amy realised Mal had been right. She wished hard she was anywhere else but here.

8

Mal — note to self. You have it bad. And you're jealous. All because she went out with that guy after all.

Mal watched her leave the restaurant with that Dean guy from the pub. He even caught a whiff of her gentle floral perfume in her wake and his gut roiled. He had a bad feeling. He wasn't usually so judgmental, so the instinct that something was off must be stronger than Elgar's lingering coat odour issues.

Amy didn't look overjoyed; in that he took solace. She walked fast, as if pleased to leave. He already knew her well enough to spot signs. The vacant look told him she was preoccupied. Why the heck hadn't she just bailed out and claimed a headache?

Amy didn't lie. It was part of her code.

Yet he'd seen the looks Dean gave

women. Amy deserved way better. Did they have anything in common?

Was he a jabbering jealous wreck?

His sister Daisy swooped like a raven.

'She's nice. And you obviously think so. Earth calling Mal!' said Daisy in a triumphant tone. That's what he got for bringing his little sister out.

Mal narrowed his eyes.

'Sorry. Did you say something?'

'Liar. Pants on fire.'

'How old are you? Five? I know her. From the café I'm helping.'

'And she's definitely fired your interest.' Her smile said she could read him like an early reader book. 'You couldn't stop gazing over and checking. And now you're watching her get into the car. Hello, Mal — I am still here! Thanks for bringing me out!'

'She owns the business I'm mentoring. And I'm not keen on the company she's keeping tonight.'

'I was thinking he looked quite handsome. Gym bunny, guns for biceps. He clearly works out.'

'Don't care. But if he lifts a finger . . . he'll be rearranging those muscles in a painful manner.'

'Mal! What are you like! One thing's for sure, if you and the lady there had babies, they'd have the wildest hair in the entire universe.'

That stopped him in his tracks. And thinking of babies he might have with Amy was enough to send his brain into a muddled mess.

His sister twirled her pasta innocently on her fork then swooped to devour it. 'Given your lack of a date in way too long, maybe this is a sign to take the lead. She's a nice-looking woman. Dip your toe back in the water. Ask her out.'

'I don't need dating advice from a girl who used to keep lolly sticks in her hair.'

'How long ago was that?'

Mal stabbed at his food like a javelin thrower out for revenge.

Why was he so riled? He hadn't realised he was in such a bad mood tonight.

But then maybe he'd be in a better frame of mind if they hadn't picked this restaurant. He should have stayed well away. Avoided local places altogether.

His sister sat back in her seat.

'Well, now Jamie and I are getting married, surely you must feel the pressure as my elder brother to settle down?'

'Ain't love grand, but really, no thanks. I'm fine.' Mal sipped his drink and realised he'd just come across as the ultimate love hater when he wasn't at all. He'd just been tied up with his career and never met the right woman. A few dates, all flops. And yes, he did fancy a night out with a woman who tweaked his interest.

'Ask her,' said Daisy. 'Your number eleven lines between your brows are showing. It's a giveaway you're cross. Get even and ask her out. Show Mr Gym Bunny you're interested and you mean business.'

She had a point. But he suspected Amy would shoot him down in flames big time.

'You're telling me I have wrinkles and now I'm supposed to listen to your advice, sis?'

'Around thirty it starts to go,' she jibed. 'By forty you'll be truly on the shelf. So wise up and make a move. Promise you'll ask her.'

Mal shook his head and acted forlorn.

'Taking dating advice from my baby sister. What's to become of me? The end is nigh.'

'You may just be glad you did, and wind up happy with a glint in your eye at the prospect of a date with the girl you fancy. Isn't that worth taking a risk for? Come on, big brother. You used to be confident and daring.'

He sipped his water and didn't taste it because the prevailing bitterness still lingered.

'Maybe.'

He wanted to. He just hadn't admitted to himself that it mattered enough for him to act.

Daisy reached out and patted his hand. 'I'm so happy you're doing up Uncle

Pat's pub. It was always meant to be this way.' She nodded to where Dean's car had been. 'So, do it. Ask her. Watch this; I'll even pay.' She took out her purse and summoned the waiter. 'She definitely looks like a woman who knows her mind so seize the day. Looks like you've got a date to plan. I give you a week to get it all set up.'

Daisy dabbed her perfectly glossed lips with her napkin then refolded it.

'I'll check up on your progress, too. Gotcha, big brother. Gotcha with a big fat G.'

★　★　★

Amy and Lorna were checking out some order issues when Mal appeared in the studio next day.

'Not interrupting, am I?'

'Of course not. I've brought Amy lunch. Just realised, I've left some stuff in the oven. I'll come back later. You two, tuck into these and I'll bring more. I'll be back.'

'She always doing Arnie impressions?' He kidded Amy. But she didn't laugh.

The horror of Dean's date was still too vivid. Her sense of humour had gone AWOL. Amy could have gaily strangled her interfering matchmaking sister too.

Just because Lorna was loved-up and happy, she figured she could spread romantic fairy dust in her wake. It made Amy's toes curl. Wasn't it bad enough she'd had the date from hell while Mal had wined and dined a new woman? If Lorna was matching them now, she'd shrivel up in mortification.

He clearly had a girlfriend. He was clearly otherwise committed.

When he'd told her before he'd happily take her out — he'd clearly meant as friends only, and because he was a newcomer in a strange place needing company.

'Sorry. I'm not great company. And Lorna is annoying sometimes.'

'That's OK. I'm terrible company too.'

'I doubt you're as bad as me.'

'Don't bet on it. I had dinner with my sister last night and all she did was take the mickey. She thinks she has a licence to tell me how to live my life. She even told me to get my hair cut.'

Inside Amy, a tiny bird took wing. Mal had been out with his sister.

'Sisters. Don't they just drive you nuts?' she confirmed with a small smile.

'So what's your bugbear?'

'I've just told Dean that we won't have any more dates. He made me feel like I'd scraped his car. Sorry. I didn't mean to moan over lunch.'

'That's OK. So you didn't enjoy your meal?'

Amy bit into her sandwich and held her hand up to talk while she ate. 'It's a nice place . . . ish.'

'Yes.'

'But even a non-date with a friend who aspires to more is not a good move. You were right. I should have listened.'

Mal smiled. 'And why would a woman as good-looking and talented as you go out on non-dates anyhow? Why don't you go out on real dates with real guys you like?'

'In case it's escaped your notice, this village isn't that big. And the queue of suitors isn't stretching down the street.'

Mal stood up, pretending to take a look, and screwed up his eyes as if trying his best to spot something and failing.

Amy slapped him playfully. 'I'm introvert through and through and there's only so much talking about pottery a man can stand.'

'I wouldn't mind.' He shrugged.

Amy's stomach flipped. The wrap she'd just bitten into was lush and tasty and melty — rather like her insides after what Mal had just said.

'You wouldn't mind what?'

'Hearing your stories. Getting to know you outside of work. Like a date, without pressure or expectation. In a mutually, I hope, likeable way. Of course that's assuming you might actually even find me worth spending time with. I know you hate my clothes sense and hair. So I'm guessing there's not much else to recommend me.'

'You're Mal Donaldson. For you, that queue stretches through Derbyshire and beyond. Eager women, not just after your dinners. Surely?'

'Maybe I just want different. Maybe I prefer pottery and introversion over posing and selfies, online profiles and celebrity boyfriend dreams.'

'What about your girlfriend, Mal?'

'Don't have one.'

'Online dating?'

'Well, I tried it with an alias. It was pretty bad. I had a few dates. Terrible. Not to be repeated. I'd rather date a plank of wood with lipstick on.'

She laughed out loud.

'You want to take me out because your online dating capabilities are dire?'

It felt good to laugh. She couldn't remember the last time she'd laughed that hard.

'Yes. I've no hope. How couldn't you fall for an intro like that? But this time we'd go to a nice pub. Somewhere for a bracing woodland walk, followed by lunch and dessert. And coffee. How about it? I may be a shark on TV but my pitches are pretty poor, all told.' Mal's handsome face was lit up from within.

'Compared to Dean's version of polished, rough and honest is very appealing.'

He slanted his eyes at her.

'You wanna date? Just the one, mind. Don't want you getting greedy. We'll be the same as we always are here. I mean, don't let my mentoring put you off. Underneath I'm a nice guy.'

'You think? I'll pick the pub, though.'

'You're bossy.' He smiled. 'I like it.'

'You just ate that wrap as if you're starved.'

'I didn't eat much last night at the restaurant.'

'Some of mine went in my handbag. Even Elgar didn't want it.'

They burst out laughing.

'Pub grub sounds just fine, and since

you've been so nice about it, you can choose the venue,' she answered.

★ ★ ★

Mal surveyed the site. The site manager marched ahead, hard hat on, taking control with a clipboard. Anyone would think this was his land.

'Of course this is only clearance phase. We're pretty pleased with where we are against schedule and I've taken the liberty of prepping a spreadsheet checklist.'

Mal scanned it. This thing must have taken some time. It would take just as long to fathom it all out and read the small print.

'Completion in four months. Still feels tight,' said Sheila beside him, incongruous in a hard hat worn with her pashmina and heels. His agent had glamour nailed, even on a construction site.

'This company always complete to deadline. With wiggle room and white space,' the site manager attested. He looked slightly affronted at the inference.

Now wasn't the time to bring up Mal's swirling doubts that kept him awake. The self-recriminations about setting up a branded establishment so close to the Chambers sisters.

They didn't know what his refurb project was yet. He didn't know how to tell them, either.

His Food Truck School and Restaurant would be a first in the country. Based here. Loud and proud. Yet now he felt like it was a rod for his back. His street food mall café jarred with The Hideaway's relaxed vibe. Because he was so close to a competitor he cared about.

'You don't look like a man on the verge of his greatest venture. I know the signs. What's up, Mal?' Sheila asked.

'I'm fine.'

'You're working too hard with the Chambers sisters. I did tell you not to take on the project but you insisted.

Isn't it all too much?'

'They're almost neighbours. That's what worries me.'

'Ten miles. Get real. Or tell them. Bring them here and get over it.'

'Your empathy chip sometimes isn't switched on, Sheila,' he challenged her.

She tossed her blonde hair over her shoulder and fiddled in annoyance with the brim of her hard hat. 'The thing about you Mal is your conscience is up at too high a frequency. You've no reason to feel responsibility here.'

Why did he see Lorna's disapproving expression in his mind's eye? Why did he imagine Amy's masked distrust as she internalised her disappointment in him with a high setting firewall?

'You're right,' he answered wishing she wasn't. 'I do need to tell them soon.'

9

Mal spotted her; the dog was a giveaway. Then again, Elgar was pretty hard to mistake, the way he ran in circles.

The bouncing child with blonde, curling hair in gumboots and a vibrant green jacket confirmed he'd found what he sought.

The urge to smile tugged at his mouth the minute he saw Amy — hair blown behind her in a curly mass while some sort of headband secured it in today's brisk breeze. Seeing her caused the concerned feeling to rise. So he forced himself on and descended the steps from the car park before he'd even rehearsed his script.

'Hey.'

Amy turned and inside something caught in his chest when she smiled. She was beautiful. Her eyes soft and gleaming, her complexion pale but with cheeks that now glowed.

He watched her turn away and hide a chuckle. 'Don't you think you should have noticed something?'

Mal looked askance, then realised his jacket was inside out. An easy mistake, given the style, but he still felt an idiot — label flapping in the breeze. He took it off and rolled his eyes.

'I did that to check if you'd catch it,' he fibbed. 'Nicely spotted, Batgirl.'

'Your honesty's as dodgy as your dress sense,' Amy kidded.

'Hi, Mal!' shouted Phoebe. 'I'm throwing sticks for Elgar. We've found some whoppers.' The girl ran ahead, teasing the dog with an enormous branch that looked as if it would need an elephant to stand a chance of retrieval.

'Actually I want to speak to you,' Mal pushed.

'Me? How come?' Amy asked.

'It's been on my mind. This conversation has.'

She stared at him with questioning eyes that made his conscience squirm.

'Sounds serious.'

'I'd like to talk to Lorna and you together. Could we meet later? Ideally I'd like to take you with me somewhere.'

She approached him swiftly.

'Nothing bad has happened, has it?'

Mal shook his head. So much for ad-libbing with the script. He wasn't doing a great job. Recognising his folly he came clean.

'I'm involved in a project locally. Recently it's started to take shape. I feel I need to be open and honest about it with you and Lorna. It's a restaurant — at my uncle's old place. I don't want you jumping to bad conclusions.'

She simply stared and didn't say a word.

The dog barked as Phoebe started singing loudly and Amy had to turn away to deal with them. When she turned back, she said, 'You don't owe us anything, Mal.'

'But I do. An eating establishment and a shop ten miles away feels too gamekeeper-turning-poacher to me.'

The look she gave him told him she wasn't exactly thrilled at the news.

'It's a free marketplace.' She shrugged.

'Yes, but you're my friends. I've felt lately I should have told you sooner. Could you possibly come and see it? I want my cards on the table with this. It's important.'

Amy took her phone from her jacket and dialled.

'Of course. I'll call Lorna now.'

Phoebe interrupted. 'Tell Amy to take me to the climbing centre, Mal. She says she needs to check its safety rules but I don't want to wait. Tell her she's being a meanie!'

Her hand on the phone waiting for Lorna, Amy answered, 'You will go. Just not today. Arranging things takes time. It's not fair to nag, Phoebe.'

He could tell by her clipped answers that he had upset her more than she was letting on, and that bothered him.

He wanted her to understand, to see that his new relationship with them at the café was the most important thing to him right now. His uncle's place mattered — but it came second.

'She's not answering and it's gone to voicemail. I'll try again.'

Amy redialled as Phoebe strode off. Mal intervened to take the strain off.

'C'mon, I'll race you in a minute, Phoebs. Once Amy's made this call, we'll have a mini Olympics. I'm a pretty good runner. Though I've seen you and you're like a speeding bullet.'

He glanced at Amy, who looked serious, then talked briefly.

'Four? When she goes off shift?'

'I'll take you both in my car.'

When Amy rang off he felt the aftermath undercurrent. Her teasing ways had gone. She'd gone inside her shell and he hated that.

'You want to run with us, Amy?'

'Not today.'

They stood in silence, both not knowing where to take things. He'd come here in an inside-out jacket to deliver a wrong-move bombshell on their fledgling trust. She'd retreated several steps, and those were both fragile and vital.

Mal closed the space and said softly, 'My project had begun long before I got involved with you guys.'

Amy walked away without another glance.

'I believe you. Thousands wouldn't. Come on, Phoebe. I want to go home now.'

★   ★   ★

Amy wanted to believe him but it smacked of *trust what I say, not what I do*. Like Jason. The memory chilled her more than her slightly damp sock from the hole in her boot.

She found her voice was low when it emerged.

'Phoebe. We need to get back.'

'You're a spoilsport.'

She knew the signs. If she rushed her, Phoebe would have a meltdown. Transitions always brought challenge and right now after Mal's revelation, she wasn't in the mood for more. She'd trusted him, grown to like him and she'd thought they'd bonded. She'd even grown to think there could be more . . . was she that gullible?

How could he get into their inner sanctum, then do this? What an idiot she was!

He was clearly a man driven by his selfish business agenda — his business angel role less philanthropic than a convenient fame tag while he built his new empire. Shame he hadn't mentioned that. She figured he should have, and inside her anger at the injustice simmered.

Even the scent from the wild roses that edged the woodland walk couldn't banish the bitterness at his foul play. Her instinct was rarely wrong. Mal was stitching them up; she could feel it.

She wanted to turn round, march back and shout at him but what good would it do? And the talk of dates and Dean and getting chummy over coffees was a sham to sidetrack her. All the while, under the table, he'd been concentrating on his business agenda to undercut them.

Phoebe broke into her thoughts.

'Amy, you have your angry face on.'

As much as Phoebe struggled with social clues, sometimes she was on the money.

'I'm just cold. Can we go?'

'Where's Mal? Isn't he coming? We could all have hot chocolate.'

'I don't know or care,' Amy replied and resisted the urge to throw a branch for Elgar as hard and far as she could just to vent the inner misgivings. 'I need to give you and Elgar a three-minute warning now. Time to go.'

Phoebe surprised her with a swift turnaround.

'I want to go now, since Mal's not here. He didn't even run like he said. Can we go to the café for a big hot chocolate?'

'Hot chocolate has never sounded better.' She snagged Phoebe's hand, fingers linking.

She wished she'd never let some Fast Eddie with slick lines make her think a world of new possibilities might exist. She should've known better and learned from the past.

*　*　*

The site visit showed in stark clarity that when Mal had told them on the car journey that his project was embryonic, he wasn't kidding. In fact he was probably talking it up. And some.

'The building should double in size. Please take these for health and safety. Humour me.'

He handed them hard hats, even though there wasn't much there except for girders that outlined the building. No workmen grafting. Diggers sat idle like steel dinosaurs with jagged teeth.

Mal got out a sheet with plans that showed glossy pictures and computer-aided predictions.

Humour him.

Amy would quite like to flounce off

and never speak to him again. Or wallop him with the end of a shovel. So much for his friendly banter, his understanding talks, coffee, chats and compassion. His praise of her skills and cow eyes. Was she so easy to get around?

He had all this in the background, knowingly, yet he'd never said a word. That made him deceitful. From the dark side. Never to be trusted again.

'This will be the cookery shop. Over to the left will be the café/restaurant. It's going to be a very different kind of dining. A mix and match with chef-led buffet stations. It's a bit like five cooking shows in one — oriental, carvery, Italian, a Nepalese curry stand. An array of dip-in-and-try stations. A new concept.'

'Sounds exciting,' said Lorna. She'd already defected. Amy sent her a warning stare. Wished she had a light sabre to zap her back onto the right side.

The site was in a place called Darwin Heights on the edge of an expansive forest, with great countryside views and woodland walks.

'Nice place,' said Lorna.

Amy wasn't ready to forgive him.

'Though you've plenty of work ahead. Surely you've had this on the boil for a while, though? Funny you didn't mention it earlier.'

Mal and Lorna looked at her. Right now she felt like detonating a few home truths.

'It was very embryonic. I've a partner who was working out the detail. It's been largely his baby. My main input is on the restaurant side.'

Amy felt as if he had all the answers. Smooth line merchants usually wriggled out of tight spots.

'A well worked-out plan. I wish you well. And seeing how much work is ahead, you'll probably want to be drawing your work with us to a close to concentrate on this.'

Did she sound bitter? Did he care?

'We aim to train cooks up to run their own food truck businesses here — with an add-on cookery short course centre. Nothing has ever been attempted on this scale before. It's as much about education as a working restaurant.'

'I like it,' said Lorna. 'Sounds like the kind of thing I'd have gone on eagerly.'

'So basically you went through our business plan and stole all the best bits for yourself?'

Mal's face reddened and he began to say something just as a phone ringtone went off. Amy knew it was hers and turned her back to answer.

A gremlin inside her was glad to have angered him. He deserved it.

But she went quiet at the news down the line.

'It's Phoebe,' Kathy told her. 'She's at the hospital. She had a fall.'

Kathy began to cry and it was clear Phoebe's mother was in a state.

'Try to stay calm. Is she stable? Will there be surgery?' Amy heard her own voice tremble.

'A friend took her to the climbing centre after you dropped her off; she was going on about wanting to go. She was harnessed, but went too high, jumped and injured her leg. My husband's not back yet and I'll struggle with the triplets, but my friend is coming to take me and help. I just wanted to let you know. Being in hospital without me will trigger her anxiety.'

'Do you want me to take you? Or go and reassure her? Maybe a familiar face might help.'

Kathy was quick to accept her offer. 'I think that would be good. And it might help if I'm late. The babies need attending to first and I've nobody to leave them with.'

Amy turned to the others. 'It's Phoebe. She's had a fall, I need to go and see her in hospital.'

'I'll take you,' Mal offered.

Immediately her ill-grace felt awkward given Mal's readiness to help.

'You don't have to do that.'

'I'm doing it whether you want it or not, Amy.'

They all headed to the car, only realising when they reached it that they were still wearing hard hats. No one commented further on the building project when they handed them to Mal, who now just looked grim.

* * *

'She's a tough kid,' Mal told her as they queued at the hospital admissions desk.

'She wanted to go to that climbing centre and I was too busy. I should have taken her.'

Mal's jaw was tensed.

'You can't do everything, Amy. We have had this conversation before, remember?'

'But I should have tried harder; instead I let her down. Tonight she was bored and I failed to cover my bad mood. She deserves better.'

'She's lucky to have you. And you couldn't have stopped anything. She's a kid, and kids learn the hard way sometimes.'

'And you know this how?'

Mal stared at her. She knew she'd hurt him.

'I'm sorry. I lash out when I'm stressed. And after today I'm a bit shaken on all fronts.'

Mal turned her to make her meet his gaze. 'You've no idea how sorry I am. Muscling in on your marketplace was never my intention and it won't happen. You're the last person I'd ever want to deceive. I wish I'd told you from day one.'

That small gesture of comfort alone made her want to cry. Not a good idea when she had come here to be a calming force.

'Phoebe Craig,' she told the woman on the desk and was given a bay area.

A minute of searching and she was outside the curtained bay. Kathy pulled back the pastel check fabric and smiled.

'I got here. Come and say hi. She's done no lasting damage. They think we won't have to stay long.' The woman's relief was clear.

Behind her, Phoebe looked so small and vulnerable on the large bed.

'Mal and Amy. It's good to see you.'

'Were you playing *Spider-man*? And you didn't wait for me?' Mal asked.

'No. I was trying to show how you'd climb if you were on an icy mountain and then you slipped.'

Mal answered. 'Hey buster. This stunt girl stuff can be bad for your health. Are you going to promise me, no more wall climbing for a while?'

'I'll try.'

Amy asked, 'How long will this take to mend?'

'We have to wait here for the X-rays to confirm things. Apparently it could have been worse,' Kathy clarified.

Amy confided, 'I had to come and see you were OK but we don't want to get in trouble for having too many at a bed. We'll see you soon.'

Mal went to give the girl a high-five.

'Glad you're OK. But no more trying to prove you can do things that are too dangerous.'

Phoebe's chin wobbled. 'I didn't mean to mess up. I've watched explorers do it on TV.'

Amy felt the dip of having been in fight or flight rush mode only for the worst to be over. She reached out for Phoebe's hand.

'Just get better as fast as you can. We can't wait to see you fit again.'

As they left the bay, a nurse stopped her.

'Am I right in thinking that's 'the Mal Donaldson'? The one who washed elephants and made a giant fish curry for a village?'

'He's your man.'

'Could you get me an autograph?'

'Sure. I'll hand it in at the desk.'

The nurse didn't want to let her go yet. 'Is he single?' She waggled her eyebrows.

'Yes. He isn't wearing a ring.'

'Our hospital charities Fun Day is a week on Saturday. If Mal Donaldson would sign some of his books, we'd be able to raffle them. Or even better, come to our fundraiser curry night as a special guest?'

'I'll ask. I'm sure he'd be persuaded.

Maybe give me a number?'

The nurse beamed and scribbled a note. 'If he's up for a curry, I'm his woman. I love a good Vindaloo too.' Grinning the nurse went off.

'He's much in demand.' Amy said under her breath. 'And he can sort his spicy private life out for himself.'

10

Mal knocked softly on Amy's apartment door, feeling like a man before the gallows. He'd underestimated how badly she'd take news of his restaurant plans.

The gap between them wasn't just gaping — it was a crevasse.

'Amy. It's Mal. Can we talk?' He asked it but he already knew he'd lost her trust.

Amy Chambers acted through life, and she did it all the time. She was almost convincing — until you got to know that look in her eyes when she thought no one noticed.

'I'm not going away until you tell me what you really think,' he stated through the wood.

'I'm really not in the mood. And I'd've thought that was obvious.'

But the key turned and the door

opened, which was a start. When he saw Amy, he was almost blown back on his heels at how much he wanted to hug her. Her hair was tousled, her face looked pale. He sensed she needed it. But no way would she let him near. She thought he was her big bad competitor now.

'Five minutes is all I need.'

'Come in, then. Five and counting.'

He followed her and motioned for her to sit. When she didn't he said. 'Please. I promise I'll say my piece and then go.'

Reluctantly she sat down. Then stopped him before he could start.

★ ★ ★

Amy wished hard she could hate him. Wished he didn't make her flesh goose-bump just being here in her tiny lounge in his checked shirt and jeans. Handsome, virile and making it all appear so effortless and cool. Smelling like a divine mix of spice and citrus.

She'd had an instinct from the start that men like Mal Donaldson didn't just walk in and start helping for no reason. They did it because it was useful to them. Like Jason had.

'Actually, you've told me enough today. I'd quite like to take my turn to talk.'

'OK.' His gaze held hers, seemingly apologetic and sincere. But looks could be deceptive. She'd learned that to her cost.

'When you came here, I was suspicious. You accused me of having issues, and I did. You see, I dated a man like you. He wasn't just a restaurateur and self-made success story; I was in love with him. I thought he loved me back. He said he did. But infatuation would have been a better description — most of it on my side.'

Mal was watching her without comment.

'He invited me into his restaurant to display my artwork. I've always dabbled and I had work on display in a library, and he saw it and contacted me. We

190

began dating. He even invited me to get involved in the restaurant with my college students. They did installations there to display their end of year exhibition and I was over the moon at the opportunity to get public recognition. It got a lot of press attention, too. Footfall for him and a new audience for my students. Win, win. But unfortunately I was just a stepping stone. I just didn't see it then.'

'I'm sorry. I'm guessing he hurt you.'

'You see, we had a famous lecturer at the college. Joanna Davenport. She was on the morning kitchen show for a while and she lectured our catering students a couple of times a month. I hadn't realised she was the target for Jason's gameplan. He needed a way in to the college. By getting me on side he got access to my superiors and invited to other events. I just helped him get access to Joanna.'

She saw Mal shake his head and his expression showed a stab of anger. Amy put up her hands.

'It's OK. I'm not looking for

sympathy. I'm explaining that I had an instinct when you came . . . *what's he about? What's in this for him? What's his prize? Where's the agenda?*'

'Please don't compare me to that.'

'That's fair. I'm not. Yet still this instinct gnawed away. Today the jigsaw piece emerged.'

'I wanted to explain to you that I've been trying to sell the restaurant I inherited from my uncle here. It held too many memories and I wasn't happy with the plans to take half of the place down and replace it, even though we got permission. I put it back on the market and wanted to sell.'

'At least I now know what you were after.'

Mal's brows knitted in frustration. 'I came here to help you. To make YOUR plans happen, not mine. But I guess I'm wasting my time trying to convince you when you've closed your mind as well as your heart. I'm sorry you were hurt. But that doesn't mean I'm out to rip you off.'

'Don't you dare turn this back on me, Mal.'

The burst of anger surprised even herself and stopped Mal in his tracks.

'You're still angry at him. And now you're angry at me because of him. And I get that — but you also have it wrong. I'm not trying to rip you off or make on this deal. In fact, tomorrow I'm pulling out of the project. It can go up for sale. Be a take-away or flats or whatever. This dissent is a sure sign that it won't work. I'll leave well alone.'

'Surely that's a bluff?'

'No. No matter what you might want to believe of me, I pride myself on being honest. It's not that big a deal. Maybe coming here with old memories was a mistake anyway.'

Amy realised she'd messed up big time. Lorna would never forgive her if she made Mal leave. And instead of laying her cards on the table with him she'd just opened up the hornet's nest and scared him away.

Mal approached her, toe to toe. So

tall, commanding and yet a gentle voice and a warm hand that took hers, said, 'Not the mentoring, Amy. My uncle's place. If it means that much to you, I'll pull out. I've messed up enough in life lately without doing it with you.'

As she looked up in incredulity, trying to process the words he'd just said — that he'd do something so massive just for her — he leaned in, cupped her face and kissed her.

Mal wasn't Jason. Mal was so very much more.

★ ★ ★

The woman who'd lately driven him crazy at work, by keeping his mind occupied with thoughts of her smile and blue eyes — had just kissed him back with as much passion as he had kissed her.

Mal almost couldn't believe it. Emboldened, standing there with her arms around him, he told her about Lucia.

'I went to France because of a woman.

I thought she was the one. I met her during filming in Spain and I fell for her, from a height. Not just because she dazzled me with her amazing family restaurant going back generations; I was overawed in all ways. To me, she was the full package. Sounds like Jason and Lucia were cast from the same mould.'

'She used you for your influence?'

'Actually, that was part of the attraction for me. Unlike other women she didn't want intrusion into her family's guarded recipe secrets. She hated media attention and downplayed my fame. It was the money that lured her. She needed a healthy bank balance to keep them afloat. I'd no idea of the trouble they were in.'

'Their restaurant wasn't successful?'

'A great many of the family relied on the business for their livelihoods. They were over-stretched. I helped them out but it was never enough; always fresh demands.'

'And what broke things?'

'When my aunt and uncle passed

away within a few months of each other I withdrew to grieve. Lucia urged me to sell my inheritance since I wasn't earning from promotional work.'

'Sounds a bit heartless.'

'And when I told her about my plans to ease off and spend time travelling solo without a film crew and to write about it, she made it clear I'd be replaced. Days later she had a new fiancé and a new cash stream.'

'You went to France to get over her? Did she repay you?'

'I did get some money back, but I was glad to have woken up. You see, my aunt and uncle were as good as parents to me after my mum and dad died. They adopted me and Daisy and I was only nine when their tour bus collided with a truck.

'They didn't survive; the only reason I wasn't there with them was I'd caught a bug before their trip and passed it to Daisy too.' Mal paused and gazed off ahead into space before continuing.

'My aunt and uncle raised us and

taught me my trade in their pub restaurant. Losing them was as hard a blow as losing my parents. I'd been concentrating so hard on work, I hadn't seen them enough before I lost them. My priority list was wrong.'

'I'm sure they'd have been proud of your success.'

'I'm still left feeling I let them down.'

Amy soothed, 'You did what you had to do at the time. And that's all any of us can say.' She reached up to tenderly kiss his cheek. 'Each night I thank my lucky stars that I woke up to being used. I'm healthy, and doing what I love now. And if it's bad stuff that's got me here — I'll still take it. Sounds like you're the same.'

'You're quite a woman, Amy Chambers.' He kissed her, lingeringly, tenderly, and relished the woman, her magnetism and the moment. 'Aren't I supposed to be the one helping you?'

'I'm sorry; I shouldn't judge all men on one bad experience. I was angry about your business plans but I had no right. Your business should be as important to you as mine is to me. You'll make your uncle's place great again, I know you will. You don't have to justify your actions to me.'

'But I do. Because I really do care what you think. You're a friend, Amy — but, as you may have worked out, I care deeply and I'm falling for you. Falling hard.'

'I can't get close, Mal — '

'You bewitch me. Have done since I met you. I can't get you out of my mind. The distance and quiet melancholy had me itching to know more. You're the most dazzling woman I've ever met.'

She smiled. 'Wow. I've never consciously dazzled in my life.'

'Well, I'm under your spell. And believe it or not I don't want a relationship. I don't need a woman messing with my mind.'

'Apologies if my dazzle inconveniences you . . . '

But her words were lost when he

pulled her closer and pressed his lips down on hers.

'All of this is the magic that starts every time you're near,' he murmured hoarsely.

She closed her eyes.

'Kiss me again, Mal. Sometimes making no sense makes the most sense of all.'

★ ★ ★

Amy woke in the wee small hours, remembering Mal had kissed her.

Mal Donaldson, career TV chef. Was he the kind of guy she should be throwing caution to the wind with? Was she just lonely after too many years of man-drought? Or star-struck? Or swept away by his concern and interest? She really needed to wake up and smell reality.

Elgar leapt out of her bed, reminding her real life still existed and some of that involved an early walk in wellies. Pulling on clothes she realised she'd have to draw back from the night before.

She had to be upfront and admit she wasn't up for more. And getting close might blur lines in their professional life. He was their big chance. Kisses might be head-turning but they were just two perhaps lonely and surprised people seeking solace.

There was no epic romance on her horizon. She just had to convince Mal of that.

★   ★   ★

Mal jogged along the woodland walk and found his pace. He'd now found his perfect track for a workout; three laps of the trim track, then two circuits of the fields at the east end of the village. He looked forward to the endorphin rush.

Just as he looked forward to getting into work later, to see Amy; he still couldn't believe his luck. He'd ask her out properly, romance her — dinner, movies, no skimping.

It was clear from the passion of their shared kisses that she felt the same. The sparks between them could power a generator.

He adored her smile, her quirky style, boundless creativity. She had so much talent and yet she was barely aware. So he'd pull out stops and sweep her away. Maybe for a night, or a weekend?

Mal jumped a gate and ran on, hurdling puddles, invigorated to his core. Today was the start of something big.

⋆　⋆　⋆

'How's the patient?'

She heard his voice before she saw him and turned slowly. In inky jeans and a checked shirt in mixed neutrals, he looked so huggable it was a crime. Especially given her conviction to regroup.

'Hi Mal. I'd like to talk. My studio's in uproar after a class so we'll have to go outside.'

'Good plan.' They went through the side door and walked to the far corner of the deserted herb garden. 'Look, last night . . . ' he began eagerly.

She shrugged, arms crossed defensively. 'We shouldn't have gone there. I'm sorry.'

'You're serious?' He took a step back.

She nodded. 'I'm jeopardising this project. Unforgivable. It was a heat-of-the-moment lapse.'

'A lapse?' She saw his jaw tense. She wished his pride didn't have to be a casualty of war.

She tried to get him to meet her gaze.

'Don't get me wrong, it was lovely. It was nice to feel the connection. I don't say that lightly . . . '

'Really?' He was close again; a step more and she'd be in his arms. He closed the space but she stepped back.

'See. This. This is what I mean. We have no room for this, Mal. Not here.'

'OK, so we take it slow? We focus on the project and only date at your pace. Your terms.'

'You have a big life beyond this place.'

'Why do you get so hung up on my career?'

'You're hugely successful. You have big dreams. I'm not in your league.'

His bewildered expression turned into a scowl.

'That does you no credit, Amy. Can't you let me be the judge of what's good for me and my future? Even my sister thinks you'd be good for me. She laid a bet for me to make a move.'

'A bet? Not sure if I'm flattered or shocked. No, I owe it to Lorna to step back.'

'Lorna would be delighted you were debunking all your 'not worthy' misconceptions!'

'Enough. Let's not argue at work. Or period.' She turned away. Her hands were shaking. Her reasoned arguments probably sounded flimsy and trite. But she just didn't want to risk letting this amazing guy into her life — this fragile skeleton of a life she'd rebuilt after being led on by a man she'd known was out of her league. She wouldn't go there again to ultimately lose him.

Mal commanded, 'One request. Let me see you tonight. Just you and me talking and see from there.'

'Is there any point? You're not listening.'

'No,' he said firmly. 'It's you who isn't listening. You've decided we can't and won't work and you're not giving things a chance. You have me as a business mentor without question. One more chance — it's all I ask,' he pushed.

'One chance,' she answered, then bit her lip, sensing she'd just lost a battle that might help him win the war.

11

Mal checked they each had a copy of his proposal then spread layouts on the table. He'd been buzzing with the potential of the full set of plans but now his glow had dimmed because of Amy's dampener. He determined to push through and focus on the proposals which he knew had stark merit.

'I had a hunch we could make better use of the meetings space. There's no pressure to follow these suggestions, this is your business — your expansion. But the architect confirms you could widen the space and functionality with the option for another dining area that doubles for functions. I hope you're as excited as I am about it.'

Amy studied his plans while Lorna enthused head-on. 'It's incredible, Mal. I can't believe we didn't think of it sooner.'

'Same company that's working on my build so there will be no charge to yourselves. By the way, I've stalled that to get moving here. Yours is top priority. Which means I have an extra team free to get cracking.'

Amy looked up, concerned.

'We can't ask you to do that.'

Mal met her gaze.

'My choice. And if you look at the executive summary I've put in a maverick suggestion.'

The women flicked over and scanned the print.

'It's an offer to become a partner, going forward. I realise this may not be your vision so it's in your hands. It's a sizeable offer. I want to be on board in this, if you'll have me. I don't expect a quick answer.'

Amy looked as if the rug she stood on had been pulled away and the sky had fallen with it.

'You — *really* — don't have to do that.'

'I want to.'

He went on to tell them all the suggestions. Finishing Amy's art workshops education space sooner than scheduled and taking on an events assistant as a temp post from the local college would help recruit regular business client lets and local group meetings. Plus a vegan high-tea initiative two days a week.

Not only did Lorna clap her hands, but Amy didn't go crazy and slam the report down.

'Why didn't we go there?'

'That's what we got a business angel for. To push. And he's done it,' said Amy. It sounded positive even if they both wore shell-shocked expressions.

'Have I gone too far?' Mal asked softly.

'Not at all.' Lorna squeezed Harry's hand. 'My interview with Stan is lined up for tomorrow. Fingers crossed. Feels like it's all coming together.'

'I really like what you're proposing,' Harry added.

Amy stood up. 'I don't need time to

consider. I think it'll work. We'll have to discuss the partner offer though; talk about a bolt from the blue. Why didn't you say before?'

'Because it wasn't something I'd planned until now. But I see it's a necessary part of what I'm doing at Darwin Heights. I need you guys with me on that one to succeed. I'm taking a few days off after today, which should give you time to think it all through.'

The sisters nodded and he held Amy's gaze as he said with loaded meaning. 'Our futures could be linked. But it's not my decision to make.'

★   ★   ★

Amy caught Mal in the car park as he was loading up the boot.

'Mal? Thank you.'

'Just doing my job. Though maybe now you'll get the message I'm in this going forward. I'm not intending to bail.'

He smiled. She wished she could

make things better between them but it wasn't that simple. She did need time to reflect and consider. Maybe it was good that he was going? So why did it hurt?

She watched him, flexing his jaw.

'I'd no idea about your partner plan.'

'The more I researched the opportunities, the more I felt part of this. As in a proper partner. But that's up to you. I thought about what you said earlier . . . I was forcing my hand about dinner and that wasn't fair. How about we do a rain check until I'm back? You need time to work out what you want. On all fronts.'

'Where are you going until Tuesday?'

He loaded up the car and locked the boot. It all felt very final and rushed.

'London. Personal stuff. My flat has sold. Work schedules to organise with my agent. Tell Phoebe I'll see her soon.'

'When will you be back on Tuesday?'

He stood with the keys in his hand.

'I'll pick you up at eight. Text me if you change your mind.'

Amy's heart whirred in her chest watching him. She didn't want him to go now. She hadn't realised it until that moment. But now he was heading off she badly wanted more time for walks . . . talk . . . and what else? What could she offer?

This was exactly what she'd tried to protect herself from. Warning him off to protect her fragile heart from disappointment.

'See you, Amy,' he called, and left her feeling more conflicted than ever.

But this time she was breathless with the recognition it was too late to hit pause on falling in love with Mal. Because she already had.

★　★　★

He'd certainly pulled out the stops. Suggestions included a college information point and a library hub. In essence it would be a fully integrated community facility at the heart of The Hideaway.

Amy couldn't quite believe he'd done that. Solved the problem of the local village's library closure and their expansion progression in one deft move. He'd already had discussions with the council, and normally that would bother her. But it didn't because he was right. The plan was right; Amy felt it in her bones. That, and gratitude.

She could imagine the space expanded with a computer area and a kids' space. A library area that would double for venue hire. He'd triumphed.

'I love it!' Lorna pronounced. 'No wonder he's so good at what he does.'

'I know. Me too. And that's why he gets the big bucks. That's why he rocks it,' Amy confided. 'You were right to have all the faith in him.'

'I'm just happy. Happy for us. This will really help us be a better, bigger deal and a real hub for the community. No reason it shouldn't fly.'

'Plus you're hoping to use the kids' play space down the line, aren't you?'

Lorna giggled. 'Course I will. But

seriously, our business angel is the best thing that's ever happened to us. We'd never have had this courage. This kind of scope takes his kind of vision.'

Amy held the plans tight.

'We have a bright future ahead and Dad would have been over the moon.'

The nervous knot inside Amy eased for the first time in a long time. And it was all Mal's doing.

★ ★ ★

Amy hadn't realised how time would drag. It wasn't as if she usually watched for Mal or mooned after him. It just felt as if he'd opened up a glittering, exploding gift box, then done a runner and left her longing for more answers.

She wanted to talk. Ask him how he'd initiated this. Explore what made him think of it. She almost considered calling him. But didn't that smack of desperation? And he was probably tied up with career-moving meetings.

Or maybe a girlfriend who'd been

missing him? He'd claimed not to have one — but could a man that gorgeous and famous really be single?

He'd become a part of the place in such a short space of time. Without him, there was a void. It didn't help that several yummy-mummy regulars at her workshop and the café had taken to asking when he'd return.

'Don't worry. He'll be back. Busy guy.'

The part-time yoga instructor who popped in for skinny lattes answered, 'Busy and dishy. Phew. How do you manage to work near him without swooning?'

'Hands in wet clay all day keeps me grounded.'

The women laughed. And Amy gritted her teeth and wished it didn't bother her that these suitors were five years her junior with pearly smiles so polar-white she needed sunglasses.

Instead, she threw herself into prepping the workshop area for refurbishment. In between projects she set herself the task of clearing cupboards, hoping Mal would be impressed.

'You don't have to get down on your knees to worship me when I drop by! Though it's flattering.'

A voice from the workshop door pulled Amy from her thoughts as she knelt to remove tools and supplies from the lower shelves.

'Dean. As if I would. But as you're here you can make yourself useful and lift this big bag for me.'

He flexed his muscles and winked.

'Ask me nicely. I'll think about it.' He smiled in a way that would rub the Cheshire cat's fur up the wrong way. 'You haven't returned texts since our date. Why should I move anything?'

Amy wished he'd taken her subtle hint.

'It wasn't a date, Dean. I told you in the car that it was best not repeated. You should go to the speed-dating night, find a like-minded girl.'

'Since when did a guy give up at the first hurdle?'

'Since he was being a gentleman and abiding by the rules.'

'Code for loser.' He sniffed. 'Ah, I get it. You only have eyes for a fancy chef with the fame and the hype. How can I compete? You kept watching him in the restaurant, I noticed.'

'Did you pop by for anything, since you're not going to move the bag?'

Dean puffed his cheeks out. 'I'll move it. But you should be nicer to me.'

He caught her hand when she turned. Amy glared a white-hot warning.

'I've tried to do this the polite way. Stop.'

He dropped her wrist as if burned.

'Where d'you want it?'

'The storage area — in the corner. So it's not in the way.'

'I know how it feels,' he said, sending her a dark look as he all but threw in the bag. 'Surplus to requirements. I know where I stand now, eh?'

He left her standing there, glad the message had been received.

* ★ ★

Amy walked into the café kitchen where her sister had just finished a lunch service. After half past two, the café's offerings had switched to drinks and home baking.

'I've just made an enemy of our delivery man.'

Lorna pulled a mocking face. 'The one that stares at you with his tongue hanging out?'

'I don't think he'll be doing that again. I told him there's no spark. He lost his pleasant veneer.'

'Best to be honest. I could've saved you the hassle. I have lots of knives in here. He wouldn't have got uppity with me.'

Amy put her hands on her hips.

'You urged me to go out with him.'

'That was before.' Her sister shrugged.

'Before what?'

Lorna screwed up her eye dramatically. 'Before a more eligible male arrived. And stole the show.'

'Don't go there.'

'For what it's worth I think you

should go for it. He's keen, you're keen. I see fireworks when he winks at you. It's better than watching a soap.'

'Are you reading tea leaves again?'

'Pregnant woman's instinct. I even dreamed of you both kissing before it happened.'

'Hogwash. How do you know that?'

'I didn't. But I just forced your hand and got evidence.' She clapped in glee. 'You should run at it like a free season ticket for vegan cake.'

'He's also out of my league.'

'I think he's very taken with what we have here. And with you. Hence the partner offer.'

'Oh yeah. I'm such a catch. Crazy artist who conjures up spectacular sculptures.'

'Red-blooded woman in need of a good time. That's the part that matters.'

'I was a bit cool before he left,' Amy answered softly. 'I've missed having him around.'

'Maybe you should try telling him what you just said to me when he's back tomorrow? That should melt the frostiness. And before you go . . . I need to have words.'

Amy bit her lip. 'Has Phoebe been cleaning her skateboard in your dishwasher again?'

Her sister took a picture from her apron pocket. And slid it towards her.

'Your scan! Aww. Beautiful!' Then she gasped. 'Is that what I think?'

Lorna nodded. 'Double trouble. Twins.'

Amy sprang from her seat and hugged her sister. 'That's fantastic. I know you've wanted this for so long. Dad would've been so happy!'

'Don't make me cry. But the point is, I haven't waited this long to have babies to miss out on it by working. And that's no reflection on how much I love this place and support it. I don't plan on being at work, Amy. I just want to be a mum. So Mal as a partner is heaven sent.

'We have Stan on board now, but the plans are going to demand more. I want you to tell him tomorrow. I also want you to decide on how we proceed — I may own this business with you but you have more of a stake in the day-to-day operations now.'

'Sis. You will always be half of this place.'

'And that's why I love you. Let's have an orange juice to celebrate. And drink to Dean's departure — I knew it would never work.'

'He actually makes noises when he drinks.'

Lorna stage whispered, 'And if he mangles our parcels it'll be a small price to pay for knowing my sister has great taste in the men she kisses.'

They laughed so hard the customers looked curiously at them, but they didn't care.

* * *

Tuesday night came sooner than she was ready for. Her nerves were playing games.

Amy took more care over her outfit than she had in years. She didn't want to look too dressed up, nor too casual. Not girly, yet not too tomboyish. She opted for a ruby shirt-waister red dress worn with a smart black leather jacket and boots.

Suddenly she felt transported back in time to when she'd acted like a woman. In her art college days she'd loved to be trendy. Tonight she had a glimpse of that younger her.

It wasn't until she was standing waiting for Mal's car to arrive that she began to second guess. Wasn't this too much? Too fitted? And while her figure could take it, maybe they'd be going to some country pub where it would be out of place. She'd just laid down her bag and started to take the jacket off to change when there was a sharp knock on the door.

Amy opened it a crack and her breath was taken away. He wore a smart grey suit and tie.

His eyes sparkled in greeting. 'You were expecting me, I hope? Hadn't forgotten?'

'Of course. Come in.' She was suddenly flushed and flustered.

'You looked at me with terror. Like you'd found the police outside with a battering ram.'

'I was going to change into something casual.'

'You look gorgeous. We're still OK to go out?'

'Yes. In fact Lorna made me promise to tell you that I've missed you. She's given me a series of lectures entitled *Amy Is In Denial And Will Tell All Tonight*. To make her stop, I agreed to be more upfront.' She felt her face flame with blushes.

'Did I ever tell you how much I like your sister?' Mal tugged her close, placing his hand gently at the small of her back to pull her into the cave of his body. He kissed her, slowly and sensuously.

'This week has been a killer wait.' He kissed her again and her brain danced on air.

He could do that again and again and

she'd never tire of it. In fact it was better than the kiss she'd been remembering on a nightly basis.

'You're quite a kisser.'

'Do you say that to all the guys?'

'I haven't kissed many. In fact I've been in a bit of a kiss drought for years.'

'In that case, we've a lot of time to make up for. Shall we forget dinner and stick with the starter?'

She laughed.

'Oh, Mal. I love it when you act crazy.'

'That makes me want to be crazier still.'

'I've missed you. I'm sorry for going cold on you before,' she confided.

'Well, I've probably missed you more. Twice I nearly got in the car to come straight back.'

They stood pressed close against each other.

'Crazy. But in a good way,' he told her. 'Come on. Let's go do the date thing. I want to ace it better than Dean. It's a personal mission.'

'I'm a guy trophy now?' she admonished him.

'You're the woman of our dreams.' His smile could calm storms and strike harmony in all discord. 'I want to show you off tonight.'

'I have more news from Lorna. They're expecting twins. It impacts on the business. We need more hands on deck. Don't suppose you'd consider filling in?'

'If you agree to wear that dress whenever I want you to, I'm sure I could be persuaded.'

'Lorna bought it for a song and then donated it to me.'

'Her loss is my gain.' He kissed her again. 'I'm not crazy for feeling this way about you.'

'We'd just be crazy to evade it,' she answered.

12

The date went more amazingly than she could ever have wished.

He took her to a rustic, thatched country pub with a tilted floor that should have made her seasick. Thankfully it didn't. It just smacked of being in a fairy story, with her own handsome prince. Amy kept waiting for a hobgoblin to appear.

'Like it?' he murmured.

'How did you find it? You're the newcomer. How come this place has evaded me?'

'Enid in the shop. Her grandmother used to live near here and she recommended it. Says it's a hidden gem not many people know of.'

'On the edge of the forest. The door looks like an elves' lair. I love it.'

'Wait for the food.' Mal grinned. 'No Michelin stars, mind.'

Their table looked onto the forest where the nearest boundary trees were strewn with lights.

'They've taken lessons from your place,' he teased.

'It's way more magical.'

'I'll get us drinks. Tell me what you fancy?'

She ordered lime and soda and Mal ordered an orange. Once settled she asked, 'How did business go in London?'

'My London restaurant has sold to a young chef — he can't wait. I'll have to sample the food when he gets up and running. A fitting goodbye. But moving on is a good plan.'

'How did it feel? To get those Michelin stars?'

'Honestly? Surreal. I didn't really do it for that. I concentrated on the menu. And then the stars came which was amazing. Imagine, my first restaurant getting the top awards on the planet.'

'And don't you miss the thrill of creating, the buzz of service?'

'I'm a chef and that won't change

wherever I work. Just like when I started, it's not about the recognition. It's about stretching yourself and sometimes that means something new.'

She took his point. 'Pass me the menu. I'm planning on choosing wisely tonight.'

He grinned at her wickedly. 'I've waited all week — I intend to savour every second.'

★ ★ ★

'I think I may struggle to walk to the car,' she admitted.

'That's OK. We can gently roll there together.'

She laughed, watching Mal lick the last of his chocolate torte and cream from his spoon.

'Thank you. For a lovely evening.'

This was so much better than the night she'd spent with Dean. The conversation flowed and Mal was both funny and entertaining. Did he realise how much he had her in the palm of his hand with his stories and anecdotes and general laid-back wonderfulness?

'Thank you. For treating me like someone normal who can actually go out on a date. By the way, the girl behind the bar admires your dress. I said you'd tell her where it came from.'

Amy smiled. 'I'd like to do this again.'

It took her some moments to realise that the sudden blast of music came from her purse.

'Sorry. Excuse me. Hello, Lorna. What's up?'

She rose, grabbing her jacket.

'It's Elgar,' she told Mal. 'He's missing. Lorna has been looking everywhere. He never goes past the strawberry field. But she's hunted everywhere. She found his collar but no dog.'

'Let's pay now,' Mal told her. 'We'll be back.'

'No rest for the wicked,' she added softly and he put his arm around her shoulder as they headed for the car.

★　★　★

'Any sign yet?' Amy fired the question at her sister as she dashed through the door but she already knew the answer from Lorna's face.

'It's dark now, it'll be hard to see. It's so unlike Elgar not to come when he's called. I've no idea where he's gone. Unfortunately the torch batteries must be flat but Harry's fetching more.'

'I'll go,' Mal said behind her. 'You aren't dressed for dog hunting, Amy.'

'Hold on and I'll change.'

Amy felt her heart wobble as he squeezed her hand rather than reply. It felt so different, to have someone else to help in a crisis.

She said softly, 'You don't have to.'

'I want to. He may be a crazy mutt but I'm pretty attached to him. We should take his lead, and his blanket so there'll be a familiar smell.'

And they left. Knight in shining armour with a torch and a handsome smile. Was there nothing he didn't rise to?

★　★　★

Mal walked up the lane for a fifth time.

'Why don't you go in, Amy? No point both of us freezing out here.'

She shivered as she paced.

'He's my dog. I'm not leaving you out here.'

'How about making us a coffee? I won't go far from the lane until you come back. I was thinking of going into the woodland next. If you rustle up another torch, too — my phone light's not as strong as I'd like.'

'I don't want to be running to A and E because you've hurt an ankle in the bushes.'

'You have such great faith in me.'

She looked crestfallen. 'It's more of a comment on how my luck's going.'

He walked towards her and took her hand in his, then pulled her to him. She smelled of oranges and something he couldn't define but already knew was uniquely Amy, and he loved it.

'We will find him. Don't fret.'

229

'You sound like me when I'm trying to pass a fib past Phoebe.'

He pulled her closer and kissed her. He lost himself in divine stalled moments with his lips locked on hers, taking energy and strength from this incredible, invigorating woman.

'We'll give it another hour. Go and make yourself useful with the coffee.'

'You're something, Mal Donaldson, you know that? Lorna's got you down as a superhero.'

'Your sister is a connoisseur.' He grinned. 'Remember that torch.'

'Apart from all the drama, tonight really was perfect.'

His heart soared. He turned the torch back on and paced up the lane again.

* * *

He might have missed it. The sound was so soft and there was hardly any movement. But a tiny muffled whine met his ears as he walked further into the trees.

'Elgar?' Mal listened, stock still.

Silence. Then a muffled tremoring whine.

He cast his torchlight on a bush ten metres to his left and a flash of brown snagged his gaze. A slight movement.

'Elgar!' A tiny bark responded.

His heart revved at turbo speed in his chest.

'Elgar! Here, boy!' Mal ran towards the blurred shape, his trousers snagging on thorns and his shoes catching in the tangled bushes. His suit would be shredded but he didn't care.

He hunkered down, unconcerned by the mud. The dog was caught fast. But shockingly, he was in a cage. His front paws were bound with rope and his muzzle was tied, though it looked to have loosened.

Mal cursed and the dog wriggled madly to try to free himself.

'Hey boy. Easy, easy.'

Mal fished for his trusty Swiss army knife doubting it would make any impact on a padlocked wire cage.

Fortunately when he tried the lock it wasn't closed. The padlock hadn't been fully locked.

'Hey. Who dared do this to our boy?' Soothing the shivering dog, Mal lifted him out. 'Easy, lad. I know two women who'll go crazy to get you home.'

The dog whimpered and yelped as Mal cut through the bindings. He carried Elgar out of the woodland, hoping he would have chance to remove the rope and ties before Amy came back.

In the lane Mal took out his mobile and called Lorna. She answered in minimal rings.

'I've found him, but please keep that quiet for now. Can Harry come out to the wood lane? There's something he needs to see.'

Mal closed the phone. 'You weren't chasing rabbits. Somebody was playing games with you. Only question is who?' The dog snuggled into his arms. 'I think you deserve a bone, boy. I think I need a glass of something warming too.'

★ ★ ★

Harry's cheery face was grave.

'So he was tied up, in a cage? On purpose?'

'Definitely.' Mal was glad that Lorna's husband concurred with his view that it would be wise to keep quiet about some of the details about how Elgar had been found.

'I worry that we'd freak them out. Having somebody kidnap your dog isn't reassuring.'

'But Amy wouldn't be happy about being kept in the dark. Poor little guy — must've freaked him out,' Harry answered.

'Especially being tied with rope. I don't intend leaving this. Not by any stretch. I'd just rather deal with it in daylight. Tomorrow we'll alert the police.'

'That sounds sensible. I'm still unsure if Amy will see it that way when she finds out. What about the cage? Surely it's evidence?'

Mal nodded gravely. 'Help me store

it somewhere tonight? Look, I'm going to take Amy her dog back. I'll play this by ear and text you.'

Harry turned towards the woodland and Mal directed him to where the cage could be found.

'We'll store the evidence in my delivery van. I know Amy would rather hear hard truths than be kept in the dark, Mal.'

'I want this cruel plotter identified. Let's give her the dog back and see how it goes from there.'

13

Amy hugged her precious pet close and stroked his fur as she listened to the full tale. Then she blurted out. 'Who on earth would do such a thing?'

Mal watched her. 'Try not to think about it. It'll only make it worse if you fixate. We'll go to the police in the morning. Can you think of any reason someone would do such a thing?'

It gave her the shivers to imagine how Elgar had felt. 'No. Of course not.'

'I worried about telling you tonight and scaring you but I couldn't undermine our relationship. I strive for complete honesty.'

Amy bit her lip. 'I'm glad you did.'

'What are you thinking?' Mal asked.

'I annoyed Dean the other day. Gave him the brush-off and it backfired. But surely he wouldn't . . . couldn't. I mean, it's pretty twisted taking somebody's dog and binding them up.'

Mal stared at her. 'What happened?'

'He left in a big huff. He couldn't have done this, though; I'm clutching at straws.'

'We should definitely go to the police and let them investigate.'

Amy shook her head in incredulity. 'I'm glad you told me. Even though it has a bad taste. Thanks for dealing with this. For walking about in the cold, dark night and not complaining once. We brought you to this sleepy backwater but you've had to jump into a few crises.'

'As it happens I'm a bit of a night walker anyway.'

'Meaning?' Amy looked at him intently.

'Insomnia. I started having difficulty getting to sleep and was prescribed pills but it persisted. When I left the public eye I was dealing with grief, but I was working hard to restore my sleep health. It's early days but I'm better than I was.'

'I'd no idea, Mal . . . '

'Some folk called it hiding out in France; I called it recovery. A backwater is exactly what I want and need. I've slept pretty well lately. Derbyshire is good for me.' Mal smoothed her hand. 'The thing lately that's helped me want to get up in the morning is you. I really like you, Amy. And that's as simple or as complicated as it gets.'

She stared at him. 'Thank you.'

'I'll stay on your couch if you agree — to keep an eye on Elgar. You won't know I'm here.'

Easy for him to say. She'd never been more aware of a man in her life.

Amy pressed a kiss on Elgar's head as he snuggled on his favourite blanket. Mal leaned over and let their heads gently fall together.

'I will happily keep watch over you,' he said softly. 'It would put my mind at rest.'

She pulled him close and gently kissed his cheek. 'I'd like that.'

His warm lips met hers and lifted her

heart to soar briefly in a place called promise. She didn't know if it was foolish or crazy, or wise . . . or meant. But she knew if she didn't go with this moment fully she'd regret it.

'You'd really buy shares in our business because you want to? You'd settle for working as a backwater café chef? Don't you think you should give yourself time and not rush into anything?'

'Trust in it. Please trust in me.'

Amy took a deep breath. Her insides were dancing.

'I do trust you, Mal. And I know you're looking out for me one hundred per cent. So I and this poor pooch are lucky to have you!' she answered. 'Let me fetch you some blankets.'

★ ★ ★

By lunchtime next day the police had visited and taken details and Elgar was back on form.

'I think I need to pamper him today,'

she told Lorna. 'He'll need hugs and lots of treats.'

'He's tough as old boots and is trying it on big style,' Lorna answered. 'You're a soft touch.'

She knew it. With dog and man both. Amy looked up and her gaze locked with Mal's. He'd just returned with supplies. The man was a Godsend to have around. She'd have to thank him somehow; another date might be called for.

'Why don't you take the rest of the day off? You did watch-duty . . . you must be shattered.'

'Maybe I don't want to?' he challenged and came close enough to snag her fingers in his. 'And I want to keep an eye on the contractors. They're here making preparations in your studio and working on planning the room expansions in synch. Should keep me out of your way. Plus I can't settle. Listen, Amy. The launch night is all in hand. We have agencies involved and subcontractors already at work. Don't fret and fuss — it's going to be an amazing success. I'm just doing something practical to stay around and help you. How about I cook an early supper and pop round later?'

'Isn't that just giving you yet more to do?'

'How does my special pasta and salad sound? I've been researching vegan cheese.'

'I'd love it.'

He was in danger of bewitching her with his social dexterity, culinary magic and his caring charm. The man multi-tasked too well.

He pointed at her. 'That's a date. Stay hungry for me.'

★   ★   ★

He arrived with a brimming casserole dish that smelled amazing when he slid off the lid. The garlic bread was ciabatta spread with pungent garlic, oil and herbs. Amy was salivating before it was on the plate.

By the time they'd got through their

bowlfuls, she was sleepy. The night before had caught up.

'That was amazing!'

'You could start on the dishes if you're really keen to repay me . . . ' He grinned.

Amy yawned widely, then looked embarrassed.

'Sorry. I'm not very good company.'

'Then you, my darling, are going to bed. I'll go soon,' Mal told her. 'Will you and your pooch be OK tonight?'

A knock sounded. But by the time Amy rose to answer, an envelope had been shoved under her door. She opened the door but already the stairway was empty. She picked it up and slit it with her finger, read it slowly and then looked up at Mal in bewildered shock.

'What is it?'

'It's from Rex, our catering assistant and HomeSmart volunteer from the homelessness charity. He's admitted to hiding Elgar — says he had good reasons and would never have hurt him. He was offered money. He says he took the wrong road. He's leaving and he's sorry for what he's done. He's left the last month's wages and more money.' She showed the wodge of notes inside the envelope.

Mal ran out with Amy behind him. 'We need to get him. Then we can sort this at the station,' he shouted over his shoulder.

'He's a good kid; we don't need to take him to the police. We just need to get him back! He's admitted the mistake. And now he's tendered his resignation. Let's just get him here to talk!'

★　★　★

Mal caught up with Rex halfway up the car park fence, on the verge of getting away. Mal kept a vice-like grip on his boot.

'This isn't how we're going to end this,' he told the trembling youth.

Rex shook his head. 'I can't let the cops take me again. I have prior convictions. Let me go. You can't make me come with you.'

He looked as if he was on the verge of dodging off again, given a glimmer of a chance.

Amy spoke softly. 'Rex. I thought you knew me well enough to trust me. No police. That won't solve things.'

'I don't want to talk about it.'

'You don't need to. And you don't need to run off and sleep rough again. I don't want you to leave your job.'

The boy turned and stared at her. 'You're just saying that. Then the police will be all over me.'

'Rex. There's no crime to answer here.'

She watched his face crumple. She knew he'd had a hard time as a teenager with drugs and gangs and had ended up homeless and sleeping rough in London. Stealing and begging to get by day to day. Would he really go back to that kind of life after proving himself an asset to her team? It felt to Amy like the ultimate failure — hers. Just as much as his.

'Tell me why it happened. Then you're free to go. If that's what you want. I'm going in to make us all a hot drink and we'll sit down. In fact — ' she laid down her mobile on the ground between them — 'I'll prove to you I'm not phoning the police by leaving this. And if you're intent on leaving you'll need it. At least you can sell it and buy food for a couple of weeks sleeping rough.'

With that she turned, leaving both Rex and Mal staring after her.

* ★ ★

Rex stared at his mug. 'Dean said he'd tell you I was nicking stuff. I wasn't; — I'd never steal from you when you've been so good to me.'

'So why did he have a hold on you? Why would Dean do that?'

'He asked me to do what he wanted or he'd tell you that. Keep the dog in the cage and then he'd get him later, he'd said. I had to put his collar on a fence so it looked like he'd gone astray. He said it was just to get you worried — the dog would be safe and he'd take him back. Make a show of finding him.'

'How much?' Mal asked. 'What did he offer?'

Amy knew he was playing bad cop to her goody-two-shoes version. But the boy deserved a break. Mal didn't know Rex like she did.

What serious issues had Rex faced for him to consider going back on the streets? HomeSmart had been a lifeline for him. He'd built a good foundation for his future life here.

'He gave me two hundred.'

'And what was he going to do with the dog?'

'He said he'd turn up at Amy's. Play the hero. That they were having relation-ship problems and he just needed a hero moment to sort things. He prom-ised Elgar would be fine.'

'Relationship problems in his delu-sional mind!' said Mal, clearly riled.

Amy took his fingers in hers under the bench.

'Dean's a plonker, Rex. I never once encouraged him. And I'm sorry he's abused you so badly.'

'Make that a devious plonker,' said Mal.

'Yes. But more plonker than criminal. Did he really think I'd fall into his arms because he found my dog? He needs lessons in the real world. And getting a life. You can't force somebody to date you or even like you.'

'So why did you need that money, Rex? You're a smart kid. You love it here — or I thought you did — and your pay is OK,' said Amy.

'Me and Abi wanna get engaged. We've been seeing each other.' The boy blushed to the tips of his ears. 'How else could I buy her a ring and show her I'm serious? She's lovely. I don't deserve her.'

For once both Amy and Mal were speechless.

Amy admonished him. 'You do so. And you should have come to me.'

Rex hunched himself up. 'I see that now. I got it wrong. It's hard to trust folk after the way my folks were.'

'You're part of this place, Rex.'

'I can't believe you still want me here after what I did. Is Elgar OK?'

'He's fine. Let the first person who hasn't made a mistake in life step forward!' said Mal, who'd switched from the bad-cop camp to the give-the-boy-a-break club. 'I've made plenty. You did the right thing in the end. That's what counts.'

'If you needed money, you should have talked to me.' Amy took the envelope from her back pocket and slid it over the table. 'I'd suggest you give that cash back to Dean; you don't want his bribery money. I'll match it and give you double for your ring. You can pay me back, on good terms. I mean, a girl with Abi's good taste will want a decent ring, won't she? She's a waitress — she wants to show it off as she takes orders!'

'And I know contacts in London who'll get you a good ring for trade. How about we talk about your plans?' Mal offered almost knocking Amy sideways with his turnaround.

She saw Rex sniff back the emotion.

'You won't be sorry. If you want me to go to the cops, I will.'

Amy looked between Rex and Mal and shook her head. 'Dog's OK. You're OK. Why would we need to, Rex? You will stay, won't you? Stan thinks you have potential. Lorna was telling me he's hoping to get you trained up — and we'll support the training. I mean, we have a few vacancies to fill in future. You'll get all the skills you need to pass with flying colours. I believe you can. Training as a chef under Mal Donaldson means you'll have the best credentials now.'

Rex leaned over the table and embraced his boss so hard the bench screeched on the tiles.

'You're amazing, Amy. I couldn't live with what I'd done.'

'You don't have to. You can take Elgar for a few walks as community service. And if he gets dirty, you're on bath duty too.' She smiled.

She felt Mal's arm around her shoulders then his deep voice added, 'You have us now, son. You have us in your corner. Don't forget it.'

14

'Where are we going, Mysterious Mal? I'm not in the mood for your games,' Amy warned, standing by the car and peering in at him. There had been so many surprises and twists in the last week she didn't need more drama.

She needed calm. But Mal was such a tease, always. It didn't help that he always pulled his adorable face to get what he wanted but Amy was wise to his tricks now.

In truth it always worried her just getting into his monster-budget car. What if she left a paint mark on the cream leather of the seat? There was usually a stray paint spatter somewhere on her! How would she afford to fix it? The thought made her wince.

'Would I ever take you somewhere bad, Amy Chambers? Trust me, it's going to be lovely and worth it. You deserve some time off. You've been burning the candle at both ends; we both have. So this is R and R.'

'I should be in the studio . . . those vases won't fire themselves! And I have some ideas for a metal piece that I can't get out of my head . . . '

'Enough art for one day. All work and no play! Stop complaining, milady. Let a man try and be gentlemanly and nice, won't you?'

'You? Nice?' Amy laughed as Mal pulled away. 'So where are we going, Mr Charming? Or is it a state secret and you're going to make me work it out, like orienteering?'

'It's called a magical mystery tour.'

And suddenly it felt really nice to be taken on a mystery trip by a famous guy who many people would pay to sit next to but who right now, only wanted to be with her.

★   ★   ★

If he was trying to blow her away Mal had succeeded. Utterly and completely.

In the romantic spot of the lot.

'Chatsworth. You should have said,' Amy exclaimed. 'I'd have got in the car like a shot.'

'Maybe I like to surprise you.'

Everyone in Derbyshire knew Chatsworth House. Not just from its location for the filming of period dramas but because of it's past heritage as the Duke of Devonshire's abode.

It felt amazing that he'd taken the time to dream this up to treat her.

'We're going to have a tour, in a while. First we wander. Enjoy the views.'

'I did that once,' Amy told him. 'The tour — with Lorna. It's quite a place.'

'Not the usual tour. This one will be special; I have contacts who can give us VIP access. But first we're doing the gardens. I've made plans.'

Amy didn't ask for more information. She sensed she wouldn't get it even if she did. Mal was enjoying his surprise too much.

She enjoyed the challenge of keeping

up with his loping pace, admiring his tall frame in smart jeans, sweater and denim jacket.

For a moment he wasn't famous Mal any more. They were just a couple out walking around a stately home, enjoying the escapism and the moment; each other's company too.

She focused all her energies into absorbing this most amazing, inspiring location. Taking in the scenery, the splendour of the house, the fountain, the grounds from the water cascade to the maze and beyond.

'I love it here.'

'So do I. I once stayed in a cottage in the grounds.'

'Lucky thing. How come?'

'I was doing a guest appearance — a dinner.'

'You get all the perks.' Amy waggled her eyebrows. 'I'm almost jealous.'

'Actually it was really hard work. Cooking for a hundred-plus covers is no easy feat.'

'Doesn't it stress you out? That much

pressure, hard work and chopping lots of things into tiny bits?'

Mal threw his head back and laughed. 'That's one way of describing my fine cuisine. Doesn't it stress you out when you have a massive metal sculpture to create to budget and erect on a hilltop?'

'Nope. I enjoy the challenge.'

'Ditto,' Mal said, reaching out and taking her hand. His gaze softened when it met hers.

She felt a surge of the now-familiar feeling she always experienced when she was near this surprising man.

They walked for a short time in happy silence and then Amy realised Mal had taken her to a quiet spot at the lower end of the lake with a perfect view of the house and the fountain in full gush.

And what a fountain! It soared high into the air in truly majestic fashion. A water feature to end all water features!

'Isn't this where Mr Darcy walked out of the water with his wet shirt in

Pride And Prejudice?' Amy teased then threw back her head and laughed. 'Don't tell me — you're going to jump in and be his stunt double. Please say yes. I can't wait!'

'Do you ever take things seriously?' Mal asked as he straightened the plaid blanket he'd found left there for them, complete with a large, promising wicker basket she assumed contained a picnic.

'Not if I can help it,' Amy answered. 'You're not exactly Mr Serious yourself. You're the chef renowned for all the banter. Don't blame me for keeping my end up.'

'Then for once, switch your sarcasm chip off and don't joke. I'm bringing you here — not to mimic Darcy — because it's probably the most artistically beautiful spot in the county of Derbyshire and as such, it's an excellent location to celebrate our joint collaborative success. And I sense you're a woman of profound good taste.

'It's also a brilliant spot for a picnic. And I've gone to a fair bit of trouble to set the whole scene. Because I want to show you that I'm serious about us.'

Amy took a seat on the blanket, somewhat chastened after his response to her teasing. Especially when a waiter appeared through the trees, carrying plates.

'Oh my goodness, this really is fancy! I thought we were just having a picnic?'

'That's just the champagne on ice in the hamper. Plus strawberries for later. No, this is a proper meal with silver cutlery and waiter service.'

'You can't drink — you're driving, Mal. Why champagne?'

His brown eyes stared into hers, dark with meaning. 'The champagne's for you. You deserve it! I'm really proud of all you're achieving and have achieved at the café, and things have been so mad recently that I've had no chance to tell you so properly. I think you've come a tremendously long way and I wanted to tell you so.'

The formally dressed waiter — presumably from Chatsworth House's famed restaurant — approached and presented a silver tray, which had little legs to act like a table. Suddenly they were sitting in their own mini outdoor high class alfresco restaurant.

They thanked the waiter and Amy watched him walk back towards the house, contemplating and taking things in, stunned into silence.

Mal removed the silver domes from their plates.

'More than a bit nice, eh?' said Mal. 'Dig in.' He motioned to plates that were as beautiful as paintings.

'Did you cook this?'

'Actually no. A friend runs the restaurant. He's very good, so we're in safe hands. I did pick the menu, however — so I hope you like it. Being vegan and all. It's just a summer salad with a vegan vegetable tart, but I hope you'll enjoy.'

And enjoy she did. She also enjoyed the plates of vegan berry cheesecake that followed. She even accepted a glass of the chilled champagne, as it would have been rude not to.

Meal over, they sat back replete and just admired their environs in contented silence.

'You been here much, then?' Mal asked, turning to watch her, the breeze off the lake lifting his dark curls from his handsome face.

'Not really. I've always enjoyed the times I have come, though.'

His hand edged closer so that their fingers brushed.

'About that tour. We're getting a special one. A good friend is taking us on the off-piste tour of the house. We get the place to ourselves.'

'That's amazing. Is everything about you special, Mal Donaldson?'

Mal shrugged. 'Only when I'm trying to impress someone. I meant what I said about serious futures, Amy. I want you to wake up and realise I am in this for the long haul.'

'Meaning me? Or my business?'

'Both. But especially you. From the heart.' His gaze locked on hers. His face showed open honesty. 'You never pick up on my hints, Amy Chambers. You're always buried away in that art lair. You're like an Old Master hiding under layers of paint — I have to keep working away at you to get through to the good stuff.'

'Charming.'

'Actually, you are. Very.' He smiled at her in a way that made her heart flip over. 'You have me hooked. And the more I peel back, the more I want to see.'

Amy didn't quite know what to say in response. She knew he liked her and she liked him back. But coming completely clean, admitting to attracting and wanting to act on it was quite another thing.

What to respond?

'And is that a good idea when we're working together? Peeling layers away and looking for more glimpses?'

'When was liking someone and doing something about it such a conscious decision, Amy? Maybe I'm just powerless in your wake. Maybe one taste isn't enough. Like with the strawberries and champagne — you're irresistible.'

She gently pushed him. 'Mal. We've only known each other a short time. As flattered as I am, we shouldn't get carried away.'

'But maybe I am already? Do you like me back — that's all I want to know. And I'm sorry if that's pushy but sometimes it pays to be open and frank.'

Amy took stock. 'Occasionally I can tolerate you well, Mr Donaldson.'

Finally the penny dropped that she was teasing him and he hooted with laughter.

'I get it. You're doing this on purpose. Emulating a scene from *Pride And Prejudice* since we're here. You're brushing me off like Lizzie did to Darcy.'

'I wouldn't dare!' But Amy giggled. 'How about we walk off this food before our tour by taking a turn around the grounds — maybe up to the top of the cascade? The view up there's fab. I might even let you hold my hand again. I quite liked it, since you're being so bold about it.'

'Sounds like a plan. I could be persuaded, now I know you really do like me. This dish has got a lot of promise. Are you serious about me too?'

Amy stared hard at him.

'I think so. I'm as sure as I've ever been — remember, I'm a tentative introvert with prudent habit from a history of being burned. But yes — I am excited about a future with you, Mal. I can't believe my luck.'

Mal reached out to take her hand and gently squeezed it.

'Come on — race you to the cascade. Last one to the top pays for ice cream later! But I'd settle for some kisses above the cascade. That romantic scene will even beat Darcy's wet shirt.'

Amy smiled coquettishly.

'Now — who's getting above himself?'

But she knew she might just let him if he tried.

15

In her newly expanded premises, Amy felt like an Empress who'd just been given the state palace keys. The finish and rework achieved took her breath away.

The proportions of the café were almost doubled, with a light, bright, airy and modern feel she adored. They'd kept the quirky edge in the existing fixtures, but added a new dimension of sharp, art-gallery polish.

To say both she and Lorna were in love with the transformation was the understatement of the century. Even though she'd had little time to idly admire it all — her hands were full.

Amy looked up at the giant jigsaw puzzle before her. She'd been up since four in the morning assembling it, so she'd be both undisturbed and unobserved.

'Is it what you hoped for?' Eric Draper asked, arriving quietly and putting down his toolbox as he removed his coat. At seven in the morning, he was a trooper, helping her out of hours.

'It's better. And I'm not boasting. Just being honest. Fancy a coffee before you start?'

'I think we should crack on, don't you?'

The *Sky Spirit* sculpture took up the centre of the new dining space, floor to ceiling. They both stood back to admire it.

The massive white wooden piece depicted a child's hand reaching up to the heavens. An adult's hand descended from the ceiling to just grasp the smaller fingers. Like a comforting divine touch interpreted on a massive scale in pale, distressed wood.

Amy smiled and hugged tight her joy at the finished article. She loved it on every level and knew it would be a talking point. Plus a perfect memorial to their father, who had loved the place so much and helped them achieve their dreams.

'I'll get started on fine-tuning the mechanism. We can have a dry run, hopefully.'

An equally intricate piece graced the entranceway to their new meetings space and library. In contrast to *Sky Spirit*, this one took up the wall that led from the dining area to the new hub.

Titled *Self Propelled*, it was a steampunk collage representation of aircraft — much of it featuring recycled aircraft parts, cogs and springs that she'd salvaged. There were small metal-skeleton aircraft that moved across the ceiling above, ranging from air balloons to zeppelins. The clockwork ticked audibly as they slowly travelled around. It reminded Amy of a grandfather clock with an aviation theme on a massive scale.

For months she'd had to work in secret at Eric's nearby workshop on her artwork through subterfuge. But now she could finally set it in motion and unveil it prior to the launch. Her first instinct was to wonder what Mal would say.

'Eric. Thank goodness you have an understanding wife,' she told her miracle worker assistant.

'I've promised her a holiday in Devon once it's all in place.'

'You deserve it.'

He was a fellow artist who had also worked as an engineer, so her project had been up his street before he'd even seen the plans. He'd been a key component in its success.

'Been looking forward to this for weeks. It's not the same on paper and in a hundred pieces. This is the bit where the fun starts.' He grinned.

'I hope you've got your other art ready to sell in the shop? I have a good feeling.'

'Of course. Couldn't pass up a chance like that. Especially with so many people coming to your launch do.'

Amy nodded. 'Mal's connections. A hundred people coming all told. Think they'll be coming for the food, though.'

'Don't kid yourself. This will really put you on the map. Be prepared for a lot of interest and commissions after the unveiling. Are we ready to give it a try out?'

Eric went to the wall and opened up the starter box. He made some final adjustments then threw her a wink.

'Cross your fingers and hope.'

The tick tock was soothing. The way the different brasses, steel and metalwork caught the lights was the real magic of the piece. They stood back, watching the mesmerising movement. It felt as if she'd woken up inside a slowly moving Victorian clock.

Amy couldn't suppress a giggle of joy.

'I love it! I could watch all day.'

'You won't have time. The cavalry will be arriving for the day ahead. We need to get the sheeting back up unless you want your secret sprung.'

'Actually, I promised I wouldn't cover it this morning. We're still closed today for fine tuning. I want them to

266

see it before the launch — so leave the tarpaulin. Fancy a coffee in my workshop before you go?'

'Sounds like an offer I can't turn down.'

Eric's grin was all the endorsement Amy needed. They'd played a blinder. And even if others hated it, as long as she and her artistic mentor were happy nothing else mattered.

Self Propelled was the landmark she'd always dreamed of. And none of it would ever have been possible without Mal. She'd never have had the courage to reach out and really go for broke otherwise. Her original sketches had been tame in comparison.

Finally, Amy knew she'd shed her past hurts and set a course for the future.

* * *

Mal felt his jaw fall. His mind and heart raced with the enormity of what was before him. And he didn't mean Lorna

Chambers' face, though he'd never seen her look more dumbstruck.

They'd not only been startled by the stunning hands sculpture that graced the centre of the new dining space — now they had a moving piece of magic to explore.

'She's really done it this time,' he heard Amy's sister say.

Mal said, 'I knew she was good — but this!'

Lorna smiled widely.

'I love it. It's wild and amazing. Like walking into a magical set from some mad inventor's mind.'

'It's show-stopping. Have you seen her today? Where is she?'

'Amy? No idea. The workshop? There's still jobs to do to prep for Friday's launch.'

'Lorna, it's totally fine. There's you and me and a full team of final year college catering students on board, who'll be assisting and waiting. We've put Stan and Rex in charge of them. I've run through everything already with them so they'll be fine.'

Lorna faked huffiness. 'You telling me I'm surplus to needs?'

'No. I'm hinting for you to take it easy, and today would be a good time to take some time to yourself.' Mal took a deep breath. 'You're pregnant. You don't need stress.'

Lorna's hands were shaking. She looked down at them and smiled wryly.

'I'm just not used to all this level of panic and attention.'

'Look at what you and your sister have achieved. Who wouldn't walk in here and be blown away and give it full marks?'

'Well. Now that you come to mention it . . . I think our Business Angel had something to do with it.'

'Your bistro and hub is going to go from strength to strength. Stan's really going to be your secret weapon, too.' Mal gave Lorna a reassuring hug. 'I do need to go and find Amy.'

Lorna turned in his arms to stare him out.

'You will look after her won't you, Mal? She needs care and reassurance.

She's had her heart broken before.'

'I know. And I'm not about to put any of that in jeopardy. She's the pinnacle of all I'd ever dared to hope for. I never imagined I could meet an Amy. She's precious.'

'OK. Go and find her. She needs a champion like you.'

Mal grinned as pure excitement raced in his veins. 'If she'll let me do it, I'll jump at the chance.'

'You'll do us proud. You already have, Mal. For a cocky celebrity business mentor you're a good man with a big heart. I'd call that deserving of my sister. And for what it's worth, I think Dad would have agreed.'

★   ★   ★

Near the fairy tree she'd created as a talking point in the woodland walk near the brook, Amy sat and took some time to breathe.

It would be OK.

Finally she could relax. Finally she

could actually believe they could do this. All was set.

With Elgar snuggled in her arms, wrapped in a blanket, she scrambled to her feet.

'We've done it. We've found a home. We've found our mojo, boy, haven't we?'

The dog looked at her as if she was talking about the contents of a butcher's shop and licked his chops.

'You like him, don't you? I like him too. Can I really trust him? Can I really take the risk? I want to ... I just promised I'd never be a fool again.'

'And yet you're standing here without a jacket, in the chilly breeze, talking to a dog. I definitely call that a sandwich short of a picnic.'

Mal's rich Yorkshire tones hauled her back to the present.

'Isn't a woman allowed any pet privacy these days?' she demanded.

'You never cease to amaze me, Amy. You know that?'

'I'm not sure which way is up right

271

now, Mal. Since you came into the café life's been a whirlwind.'

'Is that good or bad?' Mal shook his head. 'Let me take him, he looks heavy.' He took the dog, who looked like a giant burrito in a textile tortilla. 'C'mon, boy. It's no fun coming out and being cuddled like a lap dog. Let's get you down.'

The dog raced off the minute his paws touched the ground, as if Mal had read his mind.

'Does it bother you? Me being here long term? Have I moved too fast?'

'I find I can't spend enough time with you. And while I'm being sensible about it, it's all good. And it's your life — your business.'

'I now feel I have a future here, Amy. If you'll endorse that. Your artwork isn't just stunning — it's life-affirming. Only you could create such wonders. You always go above and beyond, don't you? Where do those amazing public art pieces come from?'

'Just our themes with a bit of a twist. There's something I need to share.' She gathered up Elgar's blanket and began wrapping the fringes round her fingers. 'You told me about your anxiety issues. I'm afraid I wasn't honest. You see, I have anxiety too. Sometimes I can create art and I go into crazy-creating mode like now, and I'm hard at work fourteen hours in twenty-four. Other times my mojo escapes me.

'My ADHD conflicts with an anxious side that can be debilitating. And I feel like the worst artist in the world, I've had to work hard to overcome.

'I should have been honest. That may be hard for you to deal with. It's hard enough for me. Maybe you won't like the real Amy, once you get closer?'

'Is that supposed to change my mind? Or the way I feel? Or the fact I already know I love you?'

She looked up sideways at him and shivered.

'I really want to believe that. I'm just not the impulsive type. I don't leap into the unknown. And we're just new and fragile. We've had one date.'

'Ever heard of love at first sight? It can happen.'

'This is big,' she answered. 'Big and scary.'

'You've created the most impressive sculptures I've ever seen; museum, art gallery-calibre, unique. And you invented a timepiece set in the sky that works. If that isn't big and scary and pulling it off, I don't know what is. Why are we arguing?'

'Just reasoned debating. Considering the full picture.'

'I'd rather just kiss you. I've wanted to kiss you since I saw what you did back there.'

'What's stopping you?'

'Come here.' He pulled her close to prove his feelings, his sincerity and his love. She snuggled up to his warmth and surrendered her lips to his.

'That kiss was big because that's the way my heart feels around you. And it isn't scary. The scary thing is wondering whether you don't feel it too.'

He kissed her again. And again. Until

Elgar's barking demanded attention.

'Will he always muscle in on all my big moments?' Mal grinned.

'You're starting to get our vibe,' Amy answered with a grin. 'He runs the show! Get with it!'

★　★　★

Next day Mal arrived in Amy's office with a large sealed box.

'What's in there? More surprises?' she said.

'Actually, yes. Your launch night. I've given it an extra twist.'

'Mal, I hate to steal your moment but aren't you supposed to run ideas past us for consideration and approval? I mean, I get that you're the big fancy business brain and all.' She was laughing at him and he loved that.

'Say that again. I love an ego boost.'

He stole a kiss, then opened the box and withdrew what looked like a fabric item wrapped in plastic.

'It just so happens that our launch is

happening in National ADHD week. We've been given a load of promotional gear for launch night. I wondered if some of the kids from Phoebe's club or school might come and play in the hub space on the night and we can get great photos. A charity that does sensory work will come and help. We'll do some fundraising too.'

She couldn't quite believe the man's brilliance.

Not only would Phoebe totally love to have her friends there and activity to take the edge off things, the opportunity to raise funds for such a precious charity was inspired.

Amy's eyes swam with tears and she turned away.

'I think that's a fabulous idea. How do you manage to make me fall even harder for you?'

'I have a secret — impressing you has kept me up nights since I met you. The feelings of awe is most definitely mutual.'

They kissed and she didn't want to stop.

He wiped her tears with his thumb.

'So the charity push is a goer?'

'Yes. Most definitely a yes.'

'We make a splendid team,' he told her. And she knew he was right.

16

The launch night arrived at a speed Amy barely felt ready for.

On the morning of the event she realised she hadn't planned her outfit. She hunted for her little black dress then realised it had stains that should have been dry-cleaned. Everything else just didn't suit.

'Blast! Why didn't I think earlier?'

She was almost tempted to wear the red dress from her date with Mal but that just smacked of not trying, surely?

Amy found her sister in the midst of canapé prep.

'Don't lecture me. I'm stupid not realising earlier but I've nothing to wear. Can I raid your cupboards?'

'Take the keys and don't expect me to talk right now. My outfit's on the back of the door; otherwise free rein applies. Actually can you bring my frock over in case I overrun? Most of my gear won't fit me for a while anyway. A lot is already tight around the middle.'

'Your loss is my gain. Of course I'll bring your things. Right, I'm off.' She gave her sister a brief squeeze. 'In case I don't get a chance later, you're amazing, sis. This is amazing and I sense it's all going to be good for us.'

Surprised but happy, Lorna hugged her back. 'I like the new side of you Mal brings out. I like seeing you more free and easy these days.'

'Don't say that. He already takes the credit for enough round here. See you later!'

An hour later Amy returned with an armful of clothes. She held up a lovely jacquard-embossed grey dress that was in a gorgeous fabric but very fitted.

'It's tight, but it's nice on. Whenever did you get this?'

'Don't recall. I couldn't get into that now if I jumped off the wardrobe covered in olive oil.'

'It might come to that for me yet,'

Amy returned. 'I'll put yours in the workshop. All bases covered, we hope. This is it — our big moment of truth.'

The butterflies were back with a vengeance. Though whether it was the launch or having Mal there with her, she wasn't rightly sure.

★　★　★

Mal's innards sank as reality dawned that he wouldn't make it.

As soon as he had seen the name on his phone he just knew it; this carefully planned day was all about to go disastrously wrong. He was going to get sidetracked in Daisy's drama, and he'd end up missing his most important gig ever — Amy's launch. But his sister had past history of this kind of meltdown and he couldn't abandon her.

'What's up, sis?'

'Flat tyre and now the car won't turn over either. I'm stuck on some awful creepy road in the woods and I'm scared for my life.'

'It's the middle of the day, Dais.'

'It's still creepy. I have been trying to flag down somebody to help but so far nobody's taken the hint.'

'Why haven't you called the recovery service?'

Daisy sighed. 'The signal's rubbish. Please come and help me out?'

'It sounds good enough to me.'

'Mal. You know you're better at these things than I am.'

She told him where she thought she was. Mal hoped she was right. He'd be pushing it to deal with the car then get to the launch before the VIPs and media arrived. But if his scatty sister sent him on a crazy goose chase with duff directions he'd blow it. And their sometimes tricky relationship would be maxed out.

'Hold tight. But we may have to leave your car until later.'

'You can't do that. I'm supposed to meet Jamie for dinner.'

'Then your darling Jamie may have to

collect you. Or you might have to take my car.'

She sucked in a breath.

'You'd trust me with your precious baby?'

'This is a big deal to the Chambers sisters, Daisy. I will not be late. And I won't stuff things up for them. I'm supposed to introduce the event. I have important contacts there and there's a lot of media interest. This timing isn't ideal.'

'Better get moving then. Hurry; I'm freezing. I don't have a coat.'

'I do emergency call-outs, not fashion fluffs. And if you make me late, you're going to plead to Amy for me that none of this was my fault.'

He was walking towards the car already, hunting for his keys in his pocket and hoping he'd make good time on the way there.

'This lady clearly matters. Does she know yet that you're nuts about her?'

He heard the terse tone in his own voice.

'Getting in the car now. Hang up and quit the harassment. So much for signal problems . . . '

But she was right. He really did have it bad for Amy. Mal tried not to groan as he turned the car and drove off, hoping against hope that things would work out.

He gunned the accelerator, glad of a clear road and that he knew the place well now. But as he rounded the bend, the shock didn't have time to register.

The courier van was slanted across the road, on a concealed bend.

'Woah — talk about out of nowhere!'

Mal's foot stamped hard on the brake as he shouted but he couldn't hope to miss it. He braced for impact with foot to the floor. Then pulled on the steering wheel as hard as he could even as the sound of scraping metal and glass shattering pierced the air.

He wouldn't be collecting his sister. Or presenting a launch speech now.

*   *   *

Amy paced like a lioness and that was never good.

Already a clutch of guests had arrived and more were being greeted. She'd had to be interviewed by a radio reporter and three papers, and all without Mal on hand for support. And he was due to do the official introduction launch talk soon.

She checked her watch again, seconds after the last time. There was a multi-media segment to the start of the presentation that had been professionally filmed about the mentoring programme and a stage-by-stage development film reel featuring everything about The Hideaway and HomeSmart. But now the man of the moment was missing. To an introvert like Amy this was a disaster on a Herculean scale.

'Please, please don't let this happen,' she whispered and felt her pulse rate ramping up.

Lorna grabbed her arm and frog-marched her out of the corner and into the milling guests. 'Smile, for goodness sake! Have faith. You know he's a good guy. And he'll call if there was something up.'

'So why hasn't he?' Amy scanned her phone. No calls. No texts. No clues. 'Where is he? He said he'd be here before launch time.'

She pressed his number and dialled again but the phone just rang out.

'Listen. If needs be I'll stand up and do the intro,' said Lorna. 'Don't sweat this. We're prepped and ready. We can do it just as well as Mal can. It's our project.'

'You'd do that? And why the heck would he leave us in the lurch like this?'

'If somebody has to make a stand I'm not going to sit back and let this go into meltdown around us. Nor are you. Go and talk to our guests. You are the creator of all this art — go and talk about it. OK?'

'I'll help too, Lorna,' said a small voice behind them and they turned to see Phoebe in her best grown up party dress, a shift covered in purple sequins worn with matching pump shoes. She had an ADHD T-shirt on her teddy bear.

'That's kind of you, Phoebe. But Lorna will handle it just fine. Maybe she could borrow Ted to help her along?'

'I'll need him,' said Lorna. 'Now go and mingle. Tell them Mal's held up with an unforeseen delay. Say he's bringing a VIP from the station; vamoose. When you can't find a solution, wing it is my motto.'

'You think I've known you this long without knowing that?' Amy replied with a small smile.

Wing it. The only way to go. So Amy forced thoughts of what was keeping Mal away out of her head, and did just that.

★ ★ ★

Enid from the village shop burst into The Hideaway at a run, her husband lagging behind her and looking as if he'd just run a marathon. There was blood on his shirt and his wife motioned for him to cover it.

'Where's Amy?' she asked Lorna breathlessly.

'Upstairs with the kids. They're having a photo call. What on earth's happened?'

'We need to speak to her. Urgently. The road is blocked so we couldn't come through by car. It's quite a way on foot.'

Lorna whirled round and saw that through the far window, a number of blue lights flashed in the distance. She hadn't heard anything, but then they'd all been tied up with the launch.

'What's happened?' Lorna said in clipped fight-or-flight react mode.

'We've called the police and ambulance. The road's been cordoned off. We need to find Amy — Mal's been taken to hospital. There's been a crash.'

The launch presentation was over and the guests were mingling. Lorna felt like she wanted to blow a whistle and have them gone in an instant. Despite Mal's absence, all had been well received and gone without a hitch. The smells of the amazing culinary creations still lingered, and Mal had missed it all. Waiters still mingled refilling glasses, a cheerful scene completely at odds with what she'd just discovered.

Then Lorna saw the police officers who'd just entered. She ran over and guided them towards the hub area, terrified at what she and Amy were both about to learn.

Lorna grasped her sister's arm, knowing that Amy could read her expression. She softly told her, 'Please try not to go into shock — but he's been hurt in an accident.'

Amy's fingers dug into her sister's arm so hard she had to prise them off.

'I have to go to him. Can somebody take me?'

*　*　*

An angel in a dark grey jacquard dress came into view. But she was blurry.

Was this heaven? Not exactly textbook

but not unpleasant, Mal decided.

Her hair curled in an up-style. She was a woman who held his attention like no other. Was she really an angel? No wings . . . he longed to claim her attention but he couldn't speak. Or move. And everything was white. Where was he?

Suddenly he realised it was Amy.

'Thank God you're alive.'

'I'm alive?'

'Don't tire yourself. You're getting checked out. Don't speak.'

'So I'm not in heaven?'

'No — I'm not sure how, now that I've seen the wreckage of your car. It was a miracle. And rather a shock to see it.'

Mal's voice was barely discernible.

'What about Dean? Is he OK? He had crashed into a fallen branch. I came along as an encore.'

He saw her tears, staining her cheeks and making her make-up run. He'd never seen Amy in make-up before and found he liked it.

'I believe he's in here too. You've both been really lucky. So very lucky.'

He vaguely remembered pulling the steering wheel so hard the car had whirled like something from a motor sports rally. He'd always known that car had moves. He'd just never imagined using them so dramatically and writing off his car in the process.

The doctor appeared beside them.

'Mr Donaldson. You've had quite a day.' He had a friendly grin and busy eyebrows with a life all of their own. 'You're very lucky to be alive, I hear. The emergency services tell me you left quite a scene behind you. Worthy of a soap drama.'

'Did I? I can't quite remember the full glory. Maybe it's just as well. My no claims bonus will be shot.'

The doctor laughed. 'Believe me, you're in amazing shape, though you'll need to take it easy. You have a lot of deep cuts to your arms where the car windows smashed. And your ankle's not great but we're working on that.'

'She's my angel. I'm here because of her,' Mal said and reached out to squeeze Amy's hard.

The doctor looked at Amy and nodded.

'He needs rest. And lots of grateful prayers to whoever kept him safe today. Someone did, and that's no word of a lie. His legion of adoring fans will be glad he'll have more cookery shows to film yet. Half the nurses are vying to have him on their rotas.'

Mal kept her hand in his grasp but felt his eyes drift before they'd finished talking.

★ ★ ★

Harry laid down his newspaper and withdrew his keys when he saw Amy appear in the hospital waiting room.

'I've just collected Mal's sister and dropped her off at her boyfriend's. She had a breakdown; it's been a day of road problems. Ready for me to take you home?'

Amy nodded, then suddenly went into shock mode and found there were tears she couldn't stop from falling. She shivered uncontrollably, her thoughts and emotions in a jumble.

'I can't believe him,' she muttered through chattering teeth.

'Who? Dean? He missed a heavy branch through the windscreen by inches — it landed on the van's bonnet and smashed the windscreen and made him straddle the road. Minutes later Mal met it head-on. Could have been fatal for both of them. How Mal handled the car to escape with minor scrapes and bruises is beyond belief.'

'I'm still mad at him.'

'How can you possibly be angry?' Harry challenged.

'He distracted me. Got me involved, made me take my eye off the ball. I should know better.'

Harry reached out to touch her shoulder.

'Amy, you aren't thinking straight.'

She palmed her temples. 'I need to focus. It's just like with Jason. I've kidded myself.'

'Because of Mal? He's boosted business and you're producing your best work. I've never seen you so relaxed or happy. How can you say these things? It's shock talking.'

They reached the doors and she walked outside, the cool breeze hitting her just like the realisation that hit her now. She couldn't get involved with Mal or risk heartache down the line.

'This is a big message to me that this involvement has to stop. We can't go on.'

Harry stared at her incredulously and his tone was firm and terse.

'You need to stop this. Your anxiety is talking — not the facts.'

Without further discussion he took her straight to his and Lorna's cottage.

'You're staying with us tonight. I'll go and get the dog. You need company, and to deal with the anxiety.'

'I don't want company.'

'It wasn't a question or a choice, Amy. You're in no state to be alone.'

A tiny voice inside her warned that

her brother-in-law was right. She was too immersed in old habits of guilt and self-blame to see straight.

She felt tears fall, and her shoulders shook as the pain tore inside her.

The reality of almost losing Mal today had broken the seal on her old, deep insecurities. Anxiety flooded through her once more like a dark tide she hadn't acknowledged since Jason left her. Pitied by her students . . . talked about by her peers . . . feeling no other way out existed but to leave.

Why was she risking her heart a second time when she'd found a life that was safe and productive?

She couldn't bear to love and lose again. She vowed she wouldn't let herself go there; not with Mal or anyone. Because she couldn't dare to.

17

At the edge of the airfield stood a quiet bench, in memory of an airman called Michael Menzies. She'd happened upon it one day when out with Elgar and it became a regular haunt.

'Knew I'd find you here,' Lorna said, making her jump. Calmly she sat down, placing a tall vacuum flask between them, proceeded to un-stop it and pour them a cup of hot tea.

'Am I that predictable?'

'I like predictable — it means people know where they are with you. So, yes. In a way you are. It's when you're chaotic and unpredictable that we all worry. Your anxiety takes root and gets you that way. Have you managed to calm down yet? See the truth from the fiction?' Lorna stared her down in a way that almost intimated her. 'All I know is that when you're upset you run and hide. Like a cat. You cut yourself off from those who want to support you by fleeing.'

Amy zipped up her jacket. 'I just call it needing time to process. And if this is heading towards a Mal speech, save your breath.'

'Staying away and not visiting him does you no credit. It's not fair on him. It's as if you don't trust us to help you — or maybe the person you don't trust is yourself?'

Amy rose to leave. 'Stop it, Lorna. I don't want to talk about this.'

'My point exactly.'

Amy faced her sister head-on. 'I've messed up with this. I can't trust myself to love him.'

'Messed up how? Things in life bring risk. You cannot control everything.'

Amy's tears were already running down her face. She'd cried too much lately.

'I can't give up control. I try and then I fail.'

'Surely Mal is a shining example of

somebody who proves your theories wrong? He's inspired by you; he'd do anything you asked. How can you doubt him?'

'Life will get boring here and he'll get pulled back into the fame game. He hasn't admitted it but I know. He's just passing through. The way I felt thinking I'd lost him tells me I can't cope with that down the line.'

'You could go with him on his filming trips. If I can have a baby, you can take time out.'

Elgar ran over the field towards them and ran to Lorna to be petted, unaware of the emotions being aired.

'I have too much baggage.'

'You really are getting this wrong, sis.'

'I'm going to take a few days away. I'm not telling you where; it'll be easier if he's gone when I return.'

Lorna rubbed her spiky hair into a state of mayhem. 'Sometimes, Amy, I just want to shake you. Why are you hiding?'

'I cope best alone. It's what I've learned to do.'

'Then you've learned a bad way of coping. You should go and talk to Mal and admit your fears.'

But Amy was resolute.

'You'll manage for a few days without me?'

'You'll break his heart walking out this way. He'll leave the business and we'll lose the spark and energy and support he brought with him. He's already put us both first and he doesn't deserve this treatment.'

'His career will always win.' Amy rose and turned, then whistled for Elgar. Tears blurred the way as she trudged across the airfield. Trying to blot out memories of her walks there with Mal and the hopes of a future she'd allowed to be kindled.

She wished things could be different. But this was her modus operandi and she had to protect her heart and her future.

Amy didn't even go to her friend Shelley's place first. She headed straight there. Something told her past demons had to be faced now. They'd tormented her for too long.

The restaurant that had lived on in her mind's eye since she'd left it was greatly changed, which puzzled and surprised her. No more the sleek modern interior and starry, stylish signage. Romano's Bistro had dirty windows and rubbish lay outside in the street.

Blinds were half drawn. Post gathered behind the glass doors. The sign on the door was set to closed, even though there was someone inside.

Seizing her courage, Amy rapped the door. Before she was quite ready for it Jason himself appeared, grey bags beneath his eyes and drawn in the face. It took a moment for him to recognise her and when he did she saw his open shock.

'Amy. Why are you here?'

'I need ten minutes of your time. Can I come in? Why aren't you open?'

'We're closed. Didn't you know? Or have you come to gloat?'

She followed him inside and saw that the place was a shadow of its former glory. So much so she could hardly recall the memories of the night of the big art show and the milling guests.

'What happened?'

'Bankrupt. Joanna left. I wasn't high-end enough to sustain her, apparently. Of course when her career slumped, she took it badly. So why are you here, Amy?'

'I wanted to tell you some truths.' She'd imagined it might be cathartic. Now it felt like stating the obvious much too late. 'You hurt me badly and I lost my confidence. I actually lost the ability to paint or sculpt or draw. I spent months feeling I was a failure because I honestly never saw it coming. That Joanna was who you wanted, not me. I'd believed all your lies. I'd no idea you'd used me to further your career.'

He shrugged. 'I'm a businessman, Amy. I saw a chance and I took it.'

'But I see now that was a reflection of you. You think so little of others because you have no faith in yourself. Did you love her? Or did you use her just like you used me?'

Jason's eyes screwed up and his face grew red as his temper fired up.

'She used me, more like. Bet you're delighted to find me here in such a mess, eh? She used me for my money and then ran off to pastures new when she'd sucked the business dry. I can't even afford to downsize to a café now.'

'No, Jason. It gives me no comfort at all. The only solace I can take from any of this is the fact you've just shown, by saying that, you never really knew me at all.'

He reached out to touch her hand, but she withdrew it and shook her head.

'We were good together. We could be again.'

'I don't think so. I'm not so trusting now — which is both a blessing and a curse. I wish you luck. I hope you get back on your feet. But most of all, I hope you learn not to treat people like stepping-stones who don't matter. Goodbye. That's all I wanted to say.'

With that Amy picked up her bag, turned on her heel and left. She only wished she'd got the words out years before.

And now she had food for thought; was she going to let her past stay a curse? Or was she going to take a new road?

★　★　★

The magazine cover ensnared her attention in the rack on the Tube news stand.

Mal Donaldson stood, arms crossed over a virile chest, a whisk in one hand and a chopping knife in the other. Like some Egyptian Pharaoh in chef's whites. His familiar smirk taunted her from the glossy front page, and a massive pan of

302

something delicious lay in the picture's foreground.

Amy's heart wobbled just seeing him again. Then at the bottom of the article, she saw something that made her need to moisten her lips and read again.

Mal leaves the limelight. Star's surprise burnout move away from fame.

She bought the magazine, not quite daring to read its contents yet. Stepping off the Tube escalator she stopped on the platform.

Mal was reported to have turned down a big television contract to focus on his own new Derbyshire venture with plans to train future chefs. His legion of female fans were in mourning.

She read his comments in the interview.

'Being a Mentor Business Angel has been as life-changing for me, as it has hopefully been helpful to my business mentees. Working with the Chambers sisters has been remarkable. Now I'm striking out and doing what I want at heart. Mal's Business Angel show airs on the Business Mojo Roadshow Programme on Friday at five.'

Amy scanned the words again.

Had she jumped too swiftly to assumptions about his suggested move from the limelight being lightly made? Could he really be as fully committed to the future as he'd claimed? Was the article show-sell spin?

Her stomach knotted as guilt rose at having left him in a hospital, with no word or discussion. No explanations. Immediately tempted to call him, she drew her phone from her pocket and stared at his number, hand shaking.

Right now she could barely compose her thoughts. Yet one raced through her mind.

On this one you may have got it wrong. You should have trusted him. He's not like Jason.

Amy gulped and wondered what to do next. She knew the move was hers to take. Like an ominous chess game she couldn't hope to prevail at.

But it turned out that she didn't have to wait for answers. Those were heading her way.

★ ★ ★

Shelley opened her flat door. Elgar barked in recognition, then ran straight at Amy with gusto and joy.

'Elgar. What are you doing here?'

Mal sat on Shelley's checked sofa with a cup of tea in his hand. In a leather jacket and pale blue shirt with chinos, he looked effortlessly cool and more handsome than her heart could stand. Unexpected yet somehow completely at home.

Shelley waggled her eyebrows. 'It's OK, I knew not to call the police and assume he was a dog snatcher,' said her friend with a grin. 'I watched him on *Weekend Lazy Cooks* every single morning when he hosted it. Never missed an episode. I'd go as far as to say I'm a big fan of your pal here. Pretty proud to have him grace my sofa. And if he chooses to steal your dog, I figure that's for you to sort out.'

'And you make a great cup of tea and a nice biscuit, if you don't mind me saying,' Mal answered.

Shelley beamed. 'You can come back. My home-made granola bars are good, it's true. Help yourself to another.'

Elgar barked sharply and his tail beat like crazy against the carpet.

Amy whispered, 'You said the B word. *Biscuit*. You'll have to produce one or he won't stop.'

Shelley laughed, clicked her tongue at the dog and went to fetch a dog treat. When she returned, she was carrying her coat.

'How about I take Elgar for a tour of the sights of Muswell Hill? Give you two some breathing space.' She turned back to Mal and winked.

Amy tried to calm her fluttering nerves.

'I see you two are in league against me already.'

'Never that.' Mal was on his feet

moments later and pulled her into the warm cave of his chest. 'She just knows what's at stake and is giving me a break. Someone needs to. I've had a pretty bad run of luck recently.' His gaze met hers and held it.

'What are you doing here?'

'I came by helicopter. Shimmied down a rope like James Bond. Got MI5 on this one — they're waiting with bated breath for a mission update, and they've offered Elgar a job in their dog corps,' he answered, straight-faced.

'Now you're just acting crazy again.'

He smiled, 'I like Shelley, by the way — she's a good egg. You put them in water and the good ones sink. The bad ones float. I learned that from Phoebe — they covered it in science. That kid'll go far. Only question remains — will we?'

'I know about bad eggs. I just went to see one from my past. He definitely passed the bad egg test, even now.' Amy grimaced. 'But now I've tested that out, it's made me see I've been missing out on a good one for too long. By being blind.' She looked up at him. 'I'm sorry, I was wrong. I got scared and I hid. When you had the accident it sent me into freefall. I dealt with my past today and it was a really good decision. My demons have no hold over me any more.'

He tugged her close and stole a soft kiss.

'I'm very pleased to hear that. It's progress. Talking of which, Dean and I have sorted out our differences. He came to visit me in hospital — even brought me grapes. Did you know he's a great photographer? He's promised to do you shots for a room hire and conference brochure free of charge and he'll get you a print bonus. Says it's the least he can do after nearly killing me and stealing your dog. He even encouraged me to go after you and track you down. He told me not to quit.'

As Amy watched him in wonder, Mal further explained, 'Hey. We all do daft things sometimes. You, Dean, Rex. Even me — I kidnapped your dog myself as an excuse to come and find you. Well — he looked so miserable and Lorna said he wouldn't stop howling.'

'So how did Lorna know where to find me?'

'Shelley texted. They're all worried about you.' He tugged her close. 'So was I.'

'I was the one in the wrong.'

'You were frightened. Which tells me we must matter a lot. I'd love to think that's true.'

'It is.' She let out a long slow breath. 'You matter to me more than anything else ever has. And that scared me so completely I didn't know how to face it. But I have done now. Can you forgive me and let me try to salvage what we started?'

'You need to ask?' Mal pressed his lips gently to hers. 'I couldn't hold anything against you. You're the love of my life and I thank my lucky stars that I found you. Just accept that I'm in love with you and want my whole life to revolve around you. And yes, it's early days, but that doesn't detract from the truth.'

'You're intent on giving up your celebrity role?'

'I'll be pretty busy in Derbyshire. And I still have some books and plans up my sleeve. I won't go totally to seed, buy a pipe or raise ferrets.'

Amy took in a deep breath and stepped closer.

'Please forgive me. Elgar told me you were worth trusting. At first I didn't believe him,' she admitted. 'Always trust the dog.'

Mal smiled sweetly.

'So are you ready to go home yet? Ready to hide away with me for a while?'

'Keep persuading me,' she answered as he pulled her down onto the sofa.

* * *

'You look sensational, sis,' Lorna told her. 'And you're wearing Mum's wedding necklace.'

'I am. You wore it. Now it's my turn. Do you think they'd have liked him? Mum and Dad?' Amy asked. Her heart was full of pre-wedding nerves and love and emotional mayhem.

'More than liked. We all do. He's the one!' breathed Lorna. 'Now you're as happy as I am, and I'm so content I could cry!'

'Try not to. Your make up is amazing. Shame to spoil it!'

'It's nearly time, Amy. Don't worry about wobbling on your heels. Head high and go for it! Big entrance!'

Lorna squeezed her hands and then left her to stare in the mirror for a moment.

Taking steady breaths, Amy went to the top of the stairs then stood surveying her business baby from above like a queen. The café's fairy lights had never looked brighter or more beautiful. A magical evening wedding with her nearest and dearest people had always been her dream. And now she was living it.

As she came downstairs in her silver vintage gown, she realised just what Mal had brought into her life.

Laughter; there was now so much happiness in the place her heart was full to bursting. A magical sprinkling of sophistication that told her they'd somehow up-classed their offering. New faces — thanks to Mal they'd widened the business. New chefs on board with fresh ideas. She'd even offered space in a new studio development to a fellow artist. He'd opened her eyes to opportunities and broadened their horizons on all fronts.

Her Mal. Her beloved Mal.

Everything was different. He'd somehow enhanced what they had and made it more.

They had already won awards that were hanging outside the door. And a business award to boot. His idea of getting an admin manager on board wasn't just logical and sensible — it had been the answer to their prayers.

Mal stood at the bottom of the

wrought iron staircase holding out a hand. His grey suit brought out the colour of his eyes and the pale lilac tie matched the purple rose in his buttonhole.

She couldn't wait to wear his ring. Couldn't wait to say yes.

Now that he'd opened her eyes to a new kind of future, he'd changed her life in all ways.

And even though she'd be leaving her High Marsh hideaway home to go and live at the new place behind Mal's Derbyshire restaurant, she loved the prospect of her new life even more. They'd even talked of buying somewhere abroad and living a rustic life taking students in for art and gastronomic retreats. Bring it on!

Vows over, nerves vanished, their guests cheering, Amy stared up into her new husband's eyes, seeing the familiar crinkle there when he smiled.

'I never anticipated that mentoring could lead to marriage. But I'm so very glad it has,' Mal told her softly.

'Me too. And I have a feeling we were always meant to be.'

As his lips claimed hers, Amy knew she'd finally found a man who would send her every hope shooting sky-high.